W9-BRB-942

Like Magic

Elaine Vickers

HOOKSETT PUBLIC LIBRARY
HOOKSETT, NH 03106
603.485.6092
http://hooksettlibrary.org

HARPER
An Imprint of HarperCollinsPublishers

Like Magic

Text copyright © 2016 by Elaine Vickers

Illustrations copyright © 2016 by Sara Not

All rights reserved. Printed in the United States of America.

No part of this book may be used or reproduced in any manner whatsoever without written permission except in the case of brief quotations embodied in critical articles and reviews. For information address HarperCollins Children's Books, a division of HarperCollins Publishers, 195 Broadway, New York, NY 10007.

www.harpercollinschildrens.com

Library of Congress Control Number: 2016936037

ISBN 978-0-06-241431-1

Typography by Abby Dening

16 17 18 19 20 CG/RRDH 10 9 8 7 6 5 4 3 2 1

❖

First Edition

For my mom
and my daughters,
who make my life
like magic

Grace

Chapter 1

THE DAY HER best friend moved away, Grace left for the library early. She didn't want to hear the groan and growl of the moving truck as it rolled down the street, or to see Katie's face for the last time through a car window, just a tinted-out shadow of her real self. Grace wanted to feel like she was the one leaving, not the one being left behind.

So Grace grabbed a granola bar and hurried to the bus

stop. She climbed the three bus steps, right-left-right, and sat in the sixth-row window seat. She put her bag in the seat next to her, even though there was nobody to save it for anymore, and ate her granola bar in twelve tiny bites. Threes and sixes and especially twelves usually helped settle Grace's crackling nerves, but not today.

Katie's house flashed by soon after, but Grace told herself not to look. The moving truck would block her view anyway. Or else the truck would be gone, and that would be even worse.

As the bus rumbled from one stop to the next, Grace sent her mother a message. That was the rule: if you're going somewhere, call or text first, and take your phone with you. Grace always texted. The words came easier that way, even with her own mother.

I'm going to the library. By myself.

Grace knew the text wouldn't make her mother come rushing home from work or say the right words to take away a piece of Grace's hurt. She just wasn't that sort of mother. She was more the sort of mother who would tell Grace that Katie had been a nice girl, but she'd only been around for a year, and surely there were other going-into-fifth-grade girls in the neighborhood, and why didn't Grace introduce herself to those girls? Grace's mother was the sort who always had answers, but they never quite matched up with Grace's problems.

Grace leaned forward and let her hair fall in tangerine-colored curtains around her face. She thought of all the times she and Katie had sat next to each other on this very bus, of how they'd promised to grow their hair out together. What if Katie cut her hair now that she'd moved? And what if Grace never made another best friend? The fingers of Grace's old fear crept up her neck.

No. Grace sat a little straighter and gave one stern shake of her head. *I can't let it drown me again. No matter how bad today feels.*

Grace's aching eased a little once she was off the bus and standing in front of the enormous arc of the Salt Lake City Library. Here was a building of straight lines and perfect curves, of peaceful spaces and friendly librarians' faces. A building where being quiet wasn't weird, it was following the rules. The library wouldn't ever pack up and move across the country just because its dad got a job at a fancy university in Boston. Not that libraries had dads or jobs, of course, but that was the point. That's why you could count on them.

Grace turned her face upward as she stepped through the great glass doors. She let the cool air of the library brush the summer heat from her forehead. Murmuring crowds ambled around her, their words rising and disappearing long before they reached the towering ceiling five stories above.

Even though the library made Grace feel small and alone, it was just the right kind of small and alone. She walked past the row of tiny shops inside the library—the florist with her bright blooms, the artists with their paintings and pots—and made her way down the stairs, right foot first, to the place she'd spent so many after-schools and Saturdays.

The children's library.

Grace smiled as she walked beneath the shade sails that scalloped the skylights, grateful that the children's library hadn't changed while she was away. She remembered the first time she'd brought Katie here, how they'd sat together in the cozy reading attic and shared all their secrets. They'd even shared the embarrassing ones, like Grace's fear that sometimes stole her voice, and Katie's thumb sucking that had lasted past kindergarten. They'd folded paper stars and wished on them, then tucked them between the floorboards of the reading attic for safekeeping.

The memories washed over Grace in waves, returning the ache and pulling it away again. She had come to the library today to leave Katie behind, but maybe she had it backward. If trying to forget made her sad, wouldn't it be better to just let herself remember? To look for the pieces of their friendship Katie had left behind?

A hope fluttered inside Grace as she rushed to the reading attic. What if the paper stars were still here? She felt between the floorboards until she'd reached every corner, but the stars were really gone. Grace gave up. She turned away from the reading attic and toward the books.

But then Grace noticed a tiny old woman rolling a cart toward her, and the start of a smile snuck onto her lips. Hazel was here! Grace had barely ever spoken to the old librarian with the wrinkled skin and wispy white hair, but she still felt like a friend somehow.

Hazel stopped to pick up a dropped binky and tickled the baby's fat toes as she gave it back. She said something to the baby's mother that made them both laugh. Then she straightened her ID badge and started forward again, and soon she reached Grace.

"Good morning! Can I help you find a book today?"

Grace blushed. It shouldn't be hard to speak to somebody as nice as Hazel, but it was. She swallowed and urged a few words out.

"I'm just looking."

The librarian smiled as she examined Grace through her thick glasses. "Yes, but looking for what?" Her knotted fingers touched the titles on the shelf. "Adventure? Mystery? Fantasy?"

Grace shifted in her shoes. "No, thank you." Her eyes drifted back toward the reading attic. "I was looking for something else."

The librarian studied Grace. "You've lost something, haven't you, dear? Let's check the lost and found." Before Grace could protest, Hazel took her by the hand and led her to a storage room with a small desk tucked in the far-back corner. Could the paper stars be in there? Would they have seemed special enough to save?

The librarian gripped the arms of the chair and lowered herself onto the seat. She bent to open the bottom drawer of the desk. Grace knelt beside the drawer to get a better look at what was inside: mittens, Matchbox cars, headbands, bracelets, and a herd of tiny stuffed animals. Grace sifted through the drawer, but there were no paper stars. There was nothing left of Katie at the library after all.

But underneath the clutter, Grace's fingers found something flat and smooth. She gripped the edge and lifted, careful to tip all the smaller stuff back into the drawer.

"Ah," said Hazel. "I'd forgotten about the treasure box." She scooted her glasses up her nose and took a closer look. "If someone lost this, it was years ago."

Grace turned the object over. A brass lock sealed it shut, but it was clearly a book—not a treasure box. Maybe Hazel's eyesight wasn't so good. The book looked like the locked journal Katie had kept under her mattress, only bigger and older and much more mysterious. There was a picture of a compass embossed on the cover with a tiny brass arrow pointing toward the lock. It seemed to be telling Grace, *Open me up*.

Grace traced her fingers over the gold letters of the title. *AMICITIA*.

"It's Latin," said the librarian. "For friendship, I believe. I'm afraid the key must have been lost long ago, but a bright young mind might be able to figure out how to open it."

"*Amicitia.*" When Grace formed the word with barely a whisper, it tasted like magic.

A longing grew inside her, so swift and strong that she spoke again.

"May I check it out?" Grace fumbled through her bag and offered the old woman her library card.

Hazel shook her head as she took the book from Grace and turned it over. "Oh, no, my dear."

Grace's heart fell. Maybe the librarian didn't think she was trustworthy.

But then Hazel held the book toward her. "You can't check it out with your library card. No bar code, you see? What you must do is promise to bring it back soon and safe. I don't imagine the original owner will come for it, but there may be other children who would love a turn with a treasure box."

"I promise," said Grace solemnly. She took the book and slid it into her messenger bag. All the way home, she rested her hand against its leather spine. To the rhythm of the bus and of her own footfalls, Grace whispered the word, again and again:

"*Amicitia.*" Friendship. If it had found her with Katie, it could find her again.

Grace repeated the word in her mind at dinner, when her parents talked about patient profiles and tenure reviews and barely said a word to her.

Amicitia.

The word still echoed in Grace's mind late that night as she studied the book and imagined what she might find inside. Tomorrow she'd try to open it, but for tonight, it felt wonderful to savor the mystery and think that *anything* could be inside.

Grace opened the shutters and saw three bright stars, clustered together in the northeast. And because there were three stars, she made her wish three times.

Amicitia.

Amicitia.

Amicitia.

Grace

Chapter 2

OPENING THE BOOK proved to be much more difficult than Grace had imagined. For days, she studied the surface. She looked online for lock-picking solutions. She visited the secondhand store and searched through the key drawers. She even tried to open it with a tiny screwdriver and a toothpick. But nothing worked; the lock held fast.

By the end of the fifth day, Grace sat in her room, worrying and worn out with the book in her lap. She knew it was almost time to return it, "soon and safe" like she'd promised Hazel. The book would always be safe with Grace, but the "soon" part of her promise was much more difficult to keep.

When she heard her father come home from work, Grace hid the book in her top drawer, hoping she'd have one last chance to try to open it after dinner. She had just started for the stairs when the doorbell chimed.

"Sweetheart, could you get that?" her mother called.

Grace froze. She couldn't prepare herself to say the right things when she had no idea who was waiting for her out there.

The doorbell rang again. Grace took a deep breath and made her way down the stairs—right foot first as always, then four more steps to the front door. She closed her fingers around the doorknob and closed her eyes too, just for a second. *You can do this,* she thought as she struggled to keep the fear from sinking through her skin. *You are brave.*

Just as Grace turned the knob, her mother appeared

behind her and swung the door wide open. "Honestly, Grace," she muttered as Grace stumbled out of the way. She smiled at the man on the front porch and traded him two folded bills for the bag of food he held out.

The warm, sweet scent of huli-huli chicken from Grace's favorite restaurant floated in with the food, and Grace pushed her worries away as she followed it to the kitchen.

Grace and her parents smoothed their napkins across their laps and began passing the white takeout containers clockwise around the table. The sky darkened with a late-summer storm, and Grace was glad to be safe inside.

"How was your day, sweetheart?" her mother asked, just as Grace put the first bite of tender chicken and soft rice to her tongue.

Before Grace could answer, her mother's pocket buzzed. She held up one finger to Grace as she pulled out her phone. Her eyes grew wide as she read the message, then she held it up like a trophy.

"Wonderful news! Doctor Rothschild needs hip surgery!"

Grace and her father stared. Doctor Whatschild? And how was that wonderful?

Grace's mother bowed her head just a little. "Well, of course, it's terrible for him, with such a long, painful recovery ahead. But they've asked me to deliver the keynote at the Caesarean Symposium in his place!"

Grace wasn't totally sure her mom was still speaking English, but her father made the meaning clear.

"I thought you weren't going to Boston this year because it's the same weekend as my San Francisco trip," he said. "I'll be gone until that Sunday."

"I can't pass this up," her mother begged. "It's too important. I'm sure there's a way to make it work." Grace had never heard her mother sound this desperate, and it made her uncomfortable. "It was so nice when Grace actually had a friend to stay with."

The words were true—it *had* been nice—but they still stung. Grace stared down at her napkin and refolded it across her lap.

"Isn't there anyone else from school?" asked her father.

"No one," said her mother. Grace silently agreed.

Grace's father looked up from his calendar. "We could find a babysitter."

A knot tightened deep inside Grace. The thought of

having someone staying in her home—someone new she'd have to obey, someone new she'd have to speak to—was enough to make her take action. She cleared her throat before her courage faded.

"Or I could come to Boston."

Grace's parents looked at her like they'd forgotten she was there. "I'm sorry, honey," said her mother, "but that won't work. I can't just leave you alone in Boston while I'm working."

"I could stay with Katie," Grace pleaded. "She told me to come visit."

Grace's mother cut in. "Katie lives in another part of Boston, probably nowhere near my conference. Boston is much bigger than Salt Lake, you know. Don't worry, though. I'll make it work."

Grace pushed her food around with her fork as her parents' conversation switched to Massachusetts geography and back around to important meetings, feeling much safer when they never said the word "babysitter" again. Finally, when she had rearranged things enough that it looked like she had eaten, she raced up to her room and locked the door.

Raindrops thrummed on the roof and lightning threatened from the clouds above. To settle the hammering of her heart, Grace pulled her favorite book of poems from the shelf. She sat pretzel-legged on her bed, reading to herself in a hushed voice. The familiar rhythms and words eased her mind, until she came to a poem she had only ever skimmed before:

The Arrow and the Song
by Henry Wadsworth Longfellow

I shot an arrow into the air,
It fell to earth, I knew not where;
For, so swiftly it flew, the sight
Could not follow it in its flight.

I breathed a song into the air,
It fell to earth, I knew not where;
For who has sight so keen and strong,
That it can follow the flight of song?

Long, long afterward, in an oak
I found the arrow, still unbroke;
And the song, from beginning to end,
I found again in the heart of a friend.

Grace studied the poem's title, and its first line, and its tenth. The flutter of an idea rose in her heart. She grabbed the locked lost-and-found book from her top drawer and traced her finger over the compass on the cover. What if she'd had the key all along? Maybe the arrow wasn't pointing her to the key. Maybe the arrow *was* the key!

Grace grabbed tweezers from the bathroom. She held her breath as she gently wedged one end under the tip of the arrow. Then, with a pinch and a little pull, the arrow snapped free!

Now that it was resting in her hand, cool and brassy and a smallish kind of heavy, Grace knew she'd been right. It had to be the key.

When the arrowhead wouldn't fit inside the lock, Grace tried the notched tail end. This time, as she turned the arrow, the lock sprang open. She took three deep, careful breaths, and finally she dared open the cover.

A thin border of each page remained, but the rest of the book had been cut away to form a small box. A small, *empty* box, except for the message printed on the inside of the lid in perfect black lettering.

Take this treasure,
Leave one of your own,
And remember this truth:
You are not alone.

Grace checked every corner and even tried to lift the lining, but the box was empty.

Take what treasure?

Disappointment grabbed at her heart, and Grace knew she couldn't let this happen to anyone else. *A treasure box should have treasure inside, especially if you're allowed to keep it. I'll just have to fill it with treasure myself.*

On a clean piece of notebook paper, Grace copied her new favorite poem, "The Arrow and the Song," in her very best handwriting. The page fit as perfectly inside the hollow opening of the box as the arrow fit into its cover.

Grace took another piece of paper and folded it into a star. She wrote a hint for opening the box in tiny capital letters, then tucked it into the edge of the book, wishing and hoping that the next girl would find it and know how to find the treasure too. Sad as she was to give the box up, she couldn't help but be grateful that, just for a little while, it had made her feel less lost and alone.

The very next morning, Grace rode the bus back to the library. Hazel smiled at Grace when she saw the box. "Soon and safe," she said. "Thank you, my dear. Did you ever find what you were looking for the other day?"

"Not yet," said Grace, thinking of the poem and the new paper star. "But I hope I will."

Jada

Chapter 3

JADA AND HER dad had been driving on I-80 for almost a week. From now on, when people asked where she was from, she'd probably have to say I-80.

Jada liked to tell people she was from New York, even though she had moved to New Jersey when she was two years old. That's when her mom had left them to become a big-time actress. That's when she had started calling her dad by his first name for reasons she couldn't even remember. Patrick had been taking care of them both on his tiny teacher's salary ever since.

Which was why they were slowly baking themselves in an old yellow rental truck. Jada reached out the window and let the wind guide her hand into a gentle wave. She felt the sunlight on her smooth, brown skin—same as her dad's—and wondered if either of them would ever fit in again.

They'd totally cleared out their apartment, but as she listened to her belongings rattling around in the back of the truck, Jada couldn't shake the feeling she'd left something important behind. She knew she'd packed her art supplies, but what if all her art skills were stuck in New Jersey somehow? What if there was nothing in Utah that inspired her to paint?

Maybe I just feel like something's missing because I had to leave Grandma J behind. Jada and her dad had lived lots of places, but none of them had been more than an hour or two from Grandma J and the house where Patrick had grown up.

Jada ran her fingers over the micro braids her grandma had done for her just before they left. The braids were thin as her shoelaces and a little wavy, just how Jada liked them. Perfect for running your fingers down when you felt a little unsure of things, like she did about pretty much everything right now. "Those ought to last until I see you again," Grandma J had said as she tugged and twisted the tiny strands of hair. "Bet nobody in Utah can braid like your grandma." Jada had no doubt her grandma was right.

Jada had seen the way their friends and neighbors and even her grandparents had raised their eyebrows or wrinkled their noses when Patrick told them where he and Jada were moving. But Utah was where her dad's new job was, thanks to some old friend of his Jada had never even met.

"We're almost there," Patrick said. "Half an hour, tops." He nodded out the window. "This is Park City, where all the famous movie stars come for a film festival every year." He pointed off to the left. "And that's the Olympic ski jump, and the track for the first Olympic women's bobsled!"

Jada looked at the twisty track and the ski jump, bright green in summer, but her mind was stuck on the first thing her dad had said about Park City. Maybe someday her mom would become a famous movie star and then she'd come to Utah. (Seriously, they came to Utah?) Maybe

Jada wouldn't have to find a way back to New York if she wanted to see her mom again.

The truck groaned up one long, last stretch, then purred as it passed the summit. The air conditioner began to hum, and by the time they rumbled down the canyon, Jada had almost cooled down. After one last bend in the freeway, Salt Lake City spread across the valley before them.

So far, Jada didn't see how the city got its name. She had pictured a giant lake right in the middle, salty and stagnant and disgusting. But all she could see besides city was scrubby sagebrush and a deep, jungly ravine.

Jada squinted at her dad. "So where is it?"

Patrick smiled. "The house? Just a few blocks north." He eased off the freeway at an exit marked "Sugar House."

"No, the salt lake. But now that you mention it, where's the sugar house?" Utah was weird. Jada's fears were already confirmed.

"This neighborhood is called Sugar House, I guess. But let me know if you see any real sugar houses!" He stroked his scruffy cross-country driving beard. "Although we probably shouldn't stop. A house like that wouldn't be weather resistant. Plus a witch would probably live there."

Jada shivered as she imagined a cackling witch in a

candy house. "Don't joke about stuff like that! And don't forget, you promised you'd shave when we got here."

"I know, I know. As soon as I find my razor in all those boxes." Patrick pointed away from the mountains. "I think the Great Salt Lake is out there somewhere." But now that they were off the freeway and into the neighborhood, Jada couldn't see beyond the row of roofs in front of her.

The moving truck grumbled past rows of well-kept houses with perfect yards. Jada wondered whether she'd like having a house of their own. She was used to smelling five kinds of dinner as she came up the stairs after art class and trick-or-treating without having to leave their apartment building.

"Home sweet home!" Patrick said with a smile. He stopped the truck in front of a tiny, ancient house.

Jada stared out her window at the scraggly grass growing up through the driveway and the sagging front porch. Two cracked windows flanked the front door like sad, tired eyes. "This is it?"

Patrick hopped out and started to unhitch their tiny Toyota from behind the moving truck. "What do you think? I got the landlord to lower the rent because we're going to fix it up."

"Patrick, it's a dump." A stray cat crawled out from a half-dead hedge and hissed at them as it ran away. *A witch really would live here.*

"Don't think about what it looks like now," Patrick said. "Imagine what it could be!"

Jada's art teacher had always told her she had a truly awesome imagination. The trouble was, he also told her she had a keen, sharp eye. And Jada's keen, sharp eye told her this house was a disaster. Even if they fixed it up, she'd still be stuck in a weird city that called itself sugar and salt either because Grandma J was right and everybody was white, or because there was no flavor anywhere.

Later, as Jada struggled to get her mattress up the front steps, half a dozen men around Patrick's age appeared. Every one of them wore the same smile and the same haircut.

The tallest man held out a basket of apples. "Welcome to the neighborhood!" He smiled even wider to show off his extra-white teeth. "Have some apples! They're from the tree in my backyard."

Sure they are, thought Jada.

"Can we move this stuff for you?"

Jada frowned. "Move it where?"

The men laughed, and the leader spoke again. "Into your house, I'd assume."

Jada's dad stepped in before she could answer. "Actually, that would be great. It's been a long day."

Jada wouldn't let anybody else touch her art supplies, but the grown-ups cheerfully hauled almost everything else. After only an hour, all the big stuff and even the boxes were in the right rooms. The way-too-nice guys left and said to let them know if they could do anything else to help.

When Jada and her dad got sick of unpacking, they heated some soup on the stove. Jada was grateful for her first home-cooked meal in over a week, even if Campbell's from a can wasn't totally home-cooked. They sat with their soup bowls on the uncracked parts of the front porch and looked up at the mountains.

Patrick sighed. "Aren't they amazing?"

Jada had to admit it made a beautiful picture—the sharp gray edges of the mountains against the curves and colors of the late-summer clouds. But she didn't have to admit it to Patrick.

"Yeah, it's amazing. Now anytime I want to look back

toward our real home, there won't be anything stopping me. Except the Himalayas." Jada knew the Himalayas were in Asia, but it was hard to imagine that even Everest was much taller than this.

Patrick laughed. "They're called the Wasatch Mountains, I think. And you don't need to look back. Awesome school, the great outdoors, bigger house, perfect job. Everything will be better for us here, kiddo. Just wait."

Jada dragged her spoon across the bottom of her soup bowl. If she looked up now, Patrick might think she was about to cry. If she looked up now, he might be right.

He doesn't get it at all. It's not a matter of better or worse. It's just a matter of home.

Patrick let his spoon clatter against the edge of his bowl. "Yuck. That's enough of that. I'll make something good tomorrow if you help set up my classroom—your grandma gave me her secret chicken roll-up recipe. Then we'll really feel settled in." He sat up and slapped Jada's knee. "Hey, speaking of settling in, are you ready to hang it up?"

Whenever Jada and her dad moved into a new apartment, the first thing they hung on the wall was their framed print of *Brownstones*—the painting that had made Jada want to become an artist just like Jacob Lawrence. That one scene told a whole story, and Jada had studied it and loved it since she was little.

Jada's dad stood on their stained couch and pounded a nail into the wall. Then he stepped aside and handed *Brownstones* to her. "You do the honors this time."

Jada stretched her arms to grab the edges of the frame. She threaded the wire over the nail extra carefully, then straightened the picture and stepped back.

When she looked at the painting, Jada knew that the mountains wouldn't keep her from seeing everything she'd left behind. *Brownstones* opened a window to the world of bright colors and deep browns where Jada really belonged—the ladies talking, the kids playing, the brick buildings close together. And there, in the corner window, the white-haired woman who reminded Jada of her grandma.

Jada had never felt so totally alone, like she'd been kicked out to the wrong side of the canvas. Patrick's hand startled her when it dropped onto her shoulder. "It looks pretty good, doesn't it?" he asked. Jada had to agree.

Hours later, Jada lay wide awake, sweating inside her sleeping bag since she hadn't found the box that held her bedding. Patrick snored gently in the next room as thunder rumbled in the distance. Before Jada could finish wondering whether it would rain, the first drops hit the shingles. And before she could wonder whether this fairy-tale house was really made of sugar, whether it was safe to be here at all, the first drops fell from her ceiling and slapped against the foot of her sleeping bag.

The roof was leaking. *Perfect.*

Jada dumped her winter clothes out of a plastic storage bin and set the bin on her bed to catch the drips. Then she gathered her sleeping bag in her arms and snuck into her dad's room.

"Patrick, wake up."

Snores.

"Patrick, the roof is leaking."

One loud question of a grunt, then louder snores.

Jada sighed. "At least scoot over."

Patrick rolled toward the wall, and Jada seized the moment. She spread her sleeping bag on her dad's wide bed and slithered down inside.

Jada watched raindrops race down the window, hoping

her dad was right. Maybe even in this strange new town of sugar and salt, there could be great things for her too. But until her eyes finally slipped shut, all she saw were storm clouds.

Jada

Chapter 4

BY MORNING, THE storm had passed. But Jada's problems hadn't. They kept growing for hours, until even the little ones were enough to make her itchy and upset. She wiped construction dust from yet another bookshelf in her dad's new classroom.

"Patrick, I'm going crazy over here."

Patrick stared at his computer screen, picking apart another lesson plan. "Mmmhmm."

"I'm serious. I think I might cut somebody's ear off if I have to unload one more box of your classroom book collection."

Click. Click. "Mmmhmm."

"Is it time for lunch yet?"

"Mmmhmm."

Jada chucked the dust rag at her dad. She was bored and starving, and he didn't even care enough to look away from the computer. Her tongue itched for the spicy sauce from Sumah's, her grandma's favorite African restaurant. There probably weren't any African restaurants in Utah, and they probably couldn't afford anything but McDonald's right now anyway. Not until Patrick's paychecks started coming in from his new school. From *her* new school.

The new school was actually in a very old building that used to be a theater, and it was the only reason Jada had finally agreed to move. Jada's dad had promised her that the art teacher here would be phenomenal—he had actually used that word—and Jada would have better training in Salt Lake City than they'd ever be able to afford in New Jersey.

But a phenomenal art teacher didn't seem like a good enough reason for moving anymore. Not by a long shot. Jada shoved one last armful of books onto the shelf. "I'm going exploring. I know you're not really listening, but you can't say I didn't tell you."

"Mmmhmm."

Jada set out into the half-dark hallways. She took a lap around the regular classrooms, but they all seemed mostly the same and not very exciting. As she passed by her dad's classroom again, she heard another voice.

A female voice.

A fake-laughing female voice.

Jada peeked around the doorway to check out the situation. A tall, thin lady about Patrick's age balanced a plate of brownies on top of a stack of books with library labels. She had to be the librarian—glasses, boring ponytail, and a frayed blue sweater in the middle of summer.

Patrick lifted the plate from the stack of books and chomped off half a brownie in one bite. He closed his eyes and gave a big, smiling nod. The lady laughed again, but not so fake this time. She laid her hand on Patrick's arm.

Jada stalked down the hall, trying to get as far from the brownie-baking librarian lady as possible. At the end of the very last hall, light spilled from an open doorway. Jada felt the light pulling her toward it, and as soon as she stepped inside, she knew why.

She'd walked straight to the art room. A flicker of excitement jumped in Jada's belly.

She had to admit they'd done a good job. A row of windows lined the north wall, filling the room with warmth and light. Jada sat down on one of the drawing benches and breathed in the aroma of glass cleaner and air freshener. It might look like an art room, but it didn't smell like one yet. Jada's old studio classroom smelled like acrylic paint and ceramic glaze. *That* was the scent of creativity.

Jada spotted a box of brand-new paint on the counter. She grabbed a tube of crimson and twisted off the lid. *I'll just pop the seal so it smells like art in here.*

But when Jada pierced the foil, paint oozed out the top. It slithered down Jada's fingers and dripped on the counter. *Aw, shoot. Shootshootshoot.* She tried to catch it and ended up squeezing the tube even more.

Jada panicked and passed the tube to her other hand, like that might actually solve the problem. She grabbed a paper towel, but that only smeared the paint across the counter. As she reached to turn on the faucet with her paint-stained hands, a sharp voice spoke behind her.

"What are you doing?"

Jada spun to see the brownie librarian lady in the doorway. She dropped the paint tube and paper towel in the sink and curled her red-stained fingers in front of her. "I just broke the seal," she said. "And it started squeezing itself out. It wasn't my fault!"

The woman handed Jada an old, paint-stained towel. "You have to be careful. Things do that here sometimes, because of the altitude." As Jada rinsed the rest of the paint from her hands, she felt the woman watching her.

"You're Jada, aren't you? Patrick's girl?" She held her hand out—the same hand she'd put on Patrick's arm five minutes before, when she was flirting with him. "My friends call me Mel."

Jada finished wiping her hands, then stepped forward and gave the woman's hand a barely-there shake. *Just tell me your real name, because I'm pretty sure I'll never call you Mel. I'm pretty sure we won't be friends.*

Jada capped the red paint tube and tossed it back in the box. She pulled a long line of paper towels from the roll and swiped up the rest of the drips and smears. The woman was still watching her, probably trying to think of a way to get on Jada's good side so she could get to Patrick. *Eww.*

"Okay. Well, I gotta go."

The woman smiled. "Where are you headed?"

"To . . ." Jada's gaze darted to the lady's stack of books. "The library." *Not the library. Anywhere but the library! Get it together, Jada.*

"I'm headed back there myself," said Mel. She picked up the same stack of books Jada had seen her with earlier. "Can I walk with you?"

Jada had to think fast if she wanted to ditch this lady. "Um, not the school library. The city library."

Mel's green eyes got even brighter. "Oh, the city library! What a fabulous building. If I didn't have so much to do here, I might follow you there."

Patrick picked that moment to walk into the room. Mel gave him a wide, toothy smile, like she was at a librarian photo shoot. "Have fun at the city library, you two! You're going to love it."

Jada's dad made his solving-a-puzzle eyes at her. "Right, the library. Wow, is it that time already?" He hooked his arm around Jada's shoulders and pulled her

35

out of the room. "See you later, Mel. Thanks again for the brownies!"

The grateful look on Patrick's face told Jada it was time to get him as far away from the school as possible. "Can we go out for lunch today?"

Patrick held up a satchel with the school's logo on it. "I thought we could have a picnic. And apparently, you thought we could have it at the library."

"I didn't mean it! I was just trying to get rid of her."

Patrick shrugged. "I gotta get some air anyway, and the library sounds fun. I think it's only a few blocks away."

Jada felt the desert air sucking her dry with each sweaty step toward the boring old library. Except when her dad pointed out the library, it didn't look old or boring at all. With its long reflecting pool and impossible glass wall, it almost looked like a big-city modern art museum.

Jada and Patrick found a shady spot in the library's gardens to eat their lunch. They talked about the things they wanted to find in the maze of boxes—bracelets and beads for Jada, books and running shoes for Patrick. The ice-cream maker for both of them, so they could make their specialty: strawberry-peach surprise. (The surprise was that they actually agreed on the best flavor of homemade ice cream.)

When he'd finished eating, Patrick brushed the crumbs from his lap. "I'd better head back, but you take your time. You remember how to get to the school from here?"

Jada had planned to leave the library as soon as possible, but now that she was here, staying sounded better than dusting shelves and stacking books all afternoon and running the risk of meeting up with Mel. "Yeah, I can find my way around. I was raised in New York City, remember?"

Patrick rolled his eyes. "You just keep telling yourself that." He stole the last chip right from Jada's fingers, but she grabbed it back before he got it to his mouth.

"Just promise me you'll work, Patrick. And not waste your time talking to anybody."

Patrick laughed as Jada popped the chip into her mouth. "Give Mel a chance. You might as well stay on her good side."

Jada made a stink face. "Why? Is she going to be your girlfriend?"

"Probably not, but she's going to be your art teacher."

Jada nearly choked on her chip. That ultra-vanilla lady was supposed to be an artist? The way real artists dressed reflected their creativity, which meant Mel had none whatsoever. No way was she the phenomenal art teacher Patrick had promised her at this school, the one person she'd counted on to actually *get* her in this place. Jada stared at her dad. "She's the *art teacher?* Please, please tell me you're joking."

"I'm serious as a heart attack. She's a great artist, Jada, and she's the whole reason we got to come out here. If Mel hadn't helped me get this job, we'd still be stuck in Jersey." Patrick tossed her his cell phone and the now-empty satchel. "The bag's yours to keep. The phone's still mine, though. Call the school if you need me. And don't leave your mouth open like that unless you want something to build a nest in there."

Jada stared after her dad with her jaw still dropped. It was worse than she thought. Mel wasn't just making a move. She'd made *them* move, all the way across the country. This whole Salt Lake situation was Mel's fault.

Jada's dark mood led her inside the library and straight to the art section. A quick scan showed her exactly the name she was looking for, and Jada grabbed a Picasso book from the shelf. Now *this* was an artist who understood that the world was weird and messed-up. Jada stared at one page of paintings after another until she felt a gentle tap on her shoulder.

A tiny old woman with a library name tag stood next to Jada, smiling at her and peering over her shoulder through thick glasses. The woman's silvery-white hair was tied back in a bun. "Picasso?" she asked.

Maybe the old lady wasn't as blind as she looked. "Yeah, Picasso."

The librarian nodded. "I like Picasso too, when I'm feeling out of sorts. When I want to keep feeling out of sorts."

Jada would have pegged the librarian as more of a Monet or Renoir fan, more flower gardens and happy girls. The librarian paused and studied Jada. "I don't suppose you like Cassatt?"

Jada was embarrassed to admit she'd never heard of Cassatt, so she decided to fake it. "I'm not a Cassatt fan, actually. I think he's overrated."

The old lady chuckled. "You're certainly entitled to that opinion. Enjoy your Picasso, dear. Would you like to check it out? Your mother can sign you up for a library card."

Jada's jaw snuck out, but she kept her voice even. "Thanks, but no thanks."

As the librarian shuffled away, Jada stared hard at a

purple-faced Picasso lady without really seeing her at all. There were a million things wrong with this place, and one of them was that everybody assumed your family was just like theirs. Jada decided to track down the old librarian and politely tell her what happens to people who *assume* things.

Jada marched downstairs, checking between shelves and around corners until finally she spied the librarian. The old woman sat hunched over a storage room desk and pulled a beat-up book from the bottom drawer. She plucked a pin from her hair and stuck it into the lock of the book. As much as the librarian struggled, the lock didn't spring open.

Curiosity sizzled across Jada's skin. She had to get a better look at that box, maybe even see what was inside.

Finally, the librarian gave up, returning the book to the desk drawer and pushing a cart out into the stacks. Jada ducked into the computer cave until the librarian was gone, then snuck into the storage room.

The book was lighter than it should have been, and Jada didn't understand the word on the cover. *Amicitia*. Maybe it was another supposedly–famous artist she'd never heard of. She'd rather eat Patrick's leftover mash-up casserole than read a book that old and long, but the smooth cover, the sharp arrow, and the rough edges of the pages would look great if she propped it open and painted it for a still life.

Jada sifted through the drawer, looking for more cool still-life stuff. She slipped a couple of pink plastic bracelets around her wrist. Maybe she could keep them, since things in a lost and found didn't usually belong to anybody anyway.

Except the book. Any book worth locking had to belong to somebody. After she'd dug through the rest of the drawer, Jada turned back to the lock. She tried the hairpin and the corner of her fingernail. She was getting ready to pick it with her house key when she heard the librarian's voice nearby.

Without stopping to think about what she was doing, or why, Jada pushed the bracelets back into the drawer, then stuffed the book into the school satchel her dad had given her. She was racewalking straight to the exit when she heard the old librarian's voice again.

"Soon and safe, dear."

Jada spun around. The librarian was looking straight at her. She couldn't know what was in Jada's satchel.

Unless this sweet little old lady was secretly the Witch

of Sugar House. Jada squeezed the flap shut even tighter. "Excuse me?"

"You may take that home, since it was in the lost and found. But unless it's really yours, please promise you'll bring it back soon and safe." She smiled a wrinkly smile, like she wasn't even mad. "I hope you'll be able to open it. Perhaps it could inspire a painting or two. I can tell you're an artist, not just an art lover."

It wasn't a question, so Jada didn't feel like she needed to answer. The librarian really did seem a little witch-like, but not in an evil, fatten-you-up-and-eat-you-for-dinner kind of way. Just in a mind-reading, spell-casting kind of way. Jada sidestepped toward the exit.

"Soon and safe. Got it."

Jada kept wondering about the book, but she didn't dare do anything about it until later that night. When Patrick propped his feet up on a half-full moving box in front of the TV, Jada got to work. She grabbed the scraps of copper wire she'd found in the garage and hurried back to her bedroom. Then she set the book on the bed and straightened out a short piece of wire.

The end of the wire fit into the hole of the lock, but that was all it did. No matter how much Jada wiggled or twisted it, the lock didn't budge. *Maybe if I just press a little harder . . .*

Jada pinched the wire and angled it toward the center of the book, then gave a swift, hard push. But the wire hit the back of the lock, and Jada's fingers, now a little sweaty, slipped forward. When she pulled her hand away, a line of blood grew across her palm.

Jada yanked the wire from the lock and pressed the wound to her mouth. Now what? With her good hand, she held the book up to get a better look at the lock.

But something else caught her attention instead. There, stuck against the brass bar that held the book shut, was a small paper star. And on each point of the star, one word appeared in tiny, perfect letters that couldn't have been written by the old librarian's trembling hands. Jada started at the top and read the words clockwise.

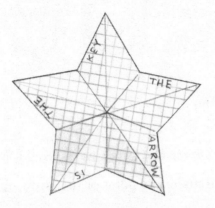

"Key the arrow is the?" With only five words, the code couldn't be hard to crack. *Maybe if I start somewhere else...* She turned the star a little to the right.

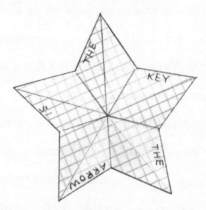

"The key the arrow is." Jada had only seen the Star Wars movies once, but that one sounded like Yoda. She turned the star a little more.

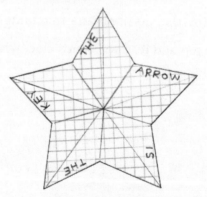

The arrow is the key! Quick as she could, Jada wedged her fingernail under the point of the arrow on the book's cover. Then she fitted the end of the arrow into the lock, hoping the librarian was right after all, that something inspiring might be here in her hands. With a twist and a satisfying click, the brass bar fell away. Jada lifted the cover a little, then swung it wide open when she saw what waited underneath.

It's not a book. It's a treasure box! She pulled out the single sheet of paper inside. *Maybe this will lead me to treasure!*

Unfortunately, the paper turned out to just be a poem, and it was a little boring the first time through. But it did plant one image in Jada's brain that stayed with her. When she read the poem again, she knew exactly what she needed to paint.

Jada grabbed her supplies and found a fresh canvas, totally relieved that all her talent and ideas hadn't been left behind in New Jersey after all. Headphones on and tunes turned up, she sketched her idea with swift, sure strokes. Hours later, when Patrick came to tell her to turn the lights out, Jada had figured out what to do with every inch of her salty-white canvas.

As she prepared her palette, a shiver snuck up Jada's neck. The librarian had been right. The box had contained the perfect inspiration for Jada's next painting. She thought of the words Grandma J had said to her, right before Jada moved away. "Everything happens for a reason, my butterfly. Keep your mind and your heart open to all the magic in the world."

Patrick had always rolled his eyes when his mom talked about anything mystical or magical, but Jada hadn't been so sure. Maybe the librarian was a little bit magic. Or maybe the book was. Or maybe both. She whispered the words inside the cover, like a spell.

"Take this treasure,

Leave one of your own,

And remember this truth:

You are not alone."

If Jada could trust those words, all she had to do was leave her own treasure in the box and she wouldn't have to feel so alone anymore.

Jada found her museum postcard copy of *Brownstones* buried deep in one of the moving boxes. She looked at the white-haired woman in the corner window. *My heart is open to this magic, Grandma J. I'm making my wish—to come home to you, and to all of this.*

The very next day, Jada brought the box back to the library with her wish and her favorite picture safe inside.

It had to work. It just had to, because Jada wasn't sure how much longer she'd last in this place.

Malia

Chapter 5

HOURS AFTER SUNRISE, the world outside Malia's window was still soaking up the night's rain. Malia had slept through the storm, but nobody could sleep through the arrival of her aunties and half a dozen of her little cousins. Their shouts and laughter snuck up the stairs and under her door until Malia had to admit she was awake for good.

How can they laugh? Don't they care that my mom's not here?

Malia slipped out of bed and locked the door. Just in time, too. Her cousins began rattling the doorknob as she climbed back under the covers.

"Hey, Malia! Are you here?" they called. "We're ready to play!"

This was not the perfect beginning Malia had imagined for her birthday. Last year, her mom had sat on the foot of Malia's bed as they'd shared strawberry waffles and remembered all the funny things Malia had done when she was little. Malia rested her hand on the empty spot where her mom should be.

"We know you're in there! Come out!"

There was shuffling and probably shoving on the other side of the door, then more knocking. Malia was the oldest cousin by far, and the little ones always squawked at her and followed her around like ducklings. She loved the attention, most of the time.

"Wait, guys," said one of the cousins. Kai, probably. "What if a zombie came in the storm? And it got Malia, and now it's waiting in there for more kids to eat?"

The mishmash of footsteps and high-pitched screams faded down the hall, so Malia decided it was safe to get dressed. She chose a bright blue T-shirt and hoped her matching blue flip-flops were in the shoe pile by the back door. Blue was her mom's favorite color, and she got to visit her mom in the hospital today.

Malia's mom had been there for over a month already, and still she could barely get out of bed without somebody worrying the baby would be born too soon. The doctors didn't dare send her home, even for her daughter's birthday.

Once Malia had brushed her teeth and tamed her almost-black hair into a braid, she took a deep breath and decided it was time to face her family. It'd be better to go down before they invaded upstairs again. But as soon as she stepped into the hallway, cousins crashed into her from every direction.

"Happy birthday, Malia! We were looking for you everywhere," said Kala. Kala always insisted on fixing her own hair, so bright fabric flowers and tufts of fuzzy black sprouted from the top of her head.

Kai laughed. "We thought a zombie got you!"

"Malia! We got you a present, and my mom made your cake since your mom is sick!" Lexi's skinny arms snaked around Malia's waist.

"Up, Mia, up?" Namea begged. Malia's tiniest cousin held her dimply hands upward and looked at Malia with pleading eyes. So, of course, Malia picked her up. And when Namea rested her warm head against Malia's chest, Malia felt strong enough to go downstairs.

Other small voices chimed in with birthday songs and wishes as Malia (and Namea, and all the little cousins) made their noisy way down to the kitchen. The counter was covered with presents and serving dishes, set down and forgotten like there was something much more important than a birthday going on in this family today.

Malia's dad and his sisters spoke in hushed voices around the kitchen table. But when the kids came through the doorway, the grown-ups jumped from their seats, trading their worried whispers for fake, cheerful voices.

"Look who woke up!" said Malia's dad. "The birthday girl herself! Doesn't she look more mature today?"

"Much more mature," agreed the aunties. They hugged Malia and wished her a happy birthday, then turned their attention to the food on the counter.

Malia's dad put his arm around her and planted a kiss on top of her head. "Your aunties will get everything ready while we're visiting Mom. And when we get home, we'll party!" He smiled and held up the cake pan. "Did you see this cake?"

Malia looked down at the sprinkled pink cake in the dark, rectangular pan. Her mom always made beautiful circular cakes and served them on a cut-glass cake stand. Soft, yellow cakes with chocolate frosting, carefully swirled in graceful arcs all around. Malia felt selfish for even thinking it, but she didn't want this flat, fallen cake with cherry frosting. She wanted her mom's cake. She wanted her mom.

"It's great," she lied. She looked at the space between the aunties and tried to smile. "Thank you for all of this," she said as they cleared spots for their food in the fridge.

Malia was relieved to trade the clamor of the house for the quiet of her dad's car. It always amazed her how differently he fit into the driver's seat than her mom did. Malia's mom was small and delicate. She had to stretch her feet to reach the pedals and her neck to see around corners. Her dad was big-boned and strong, tough enough that he'd played linebacker in college.

Malia had realized years ago that she was built like her dad. And even though she loved him a lot, she didn't exactly want to look like him. (She definitely didn't want to play linebacker in college.)

"When we get there," Malia's dad said, "I'll go grab a cinnamon roll in the cafeteria to give you and your mom a little time alone." He drummed his fingers on the steering wheel. "So, what do you want for your birthday? Besides the other half of my cinnamon roll."

Malia watched his eyes in the rearview mirror. Was he joking? He knew you were supposed to find out this stuff before the actual birthday, right?

"We can stop somewhere on our way home. How many kids get to help pick their own birthday presents?" He smiled at her hopefully in the mirror, asking her to understand. To forgive him.

"Only the luckiest ones," she said. She turned back to the window and watched the hospital grow on the horizon so he wouldn't see the tears gathering in her eyes.

Malia watched the peaks and valleys of her mom's monitors. Blood pressure a little high, but not too bad. Heart rate good. She'd ask her mom about contractions and check her feet for swelling when she woke up.

Malia sat down and rested her head against the edge of her mom's pillow. She turned her attention to the gentle rise and fall of the bump in her mom's belly. At thirty weeks, Malia's baby sister would be the size of a sweet potato now, and a sweet potato baby was still too small.

A gentle kiss landed on top of Malia's head. "Happy birthday, baby," said her mom, opening her eyes and shifting on the bed.

I won't be your baby much longer.

Malia had always soaked up the attention and love of the adults in her family. She was the first baby born on her mom's side and her dad's side, so all the grandparents and uncles and especially the aunties had been crazy about her.

Even when the little cousins had started to come along, she'd had her parents all to herself. They'd called her things like "our favorite girl" and "the best daughter in the universe."

But her parents had already stopped saying those things. Now they called her "our beautiful girl" and "the best big sister in the universe" instead. Like they had to protect a sweet potato baby who couldn't even hear or understand or get jealous. Like Malia needed one more reminder that everything was changing.

The last big change had come in the middle of third grade, when they'd moved downtown to open the family restaurant. Malia had begged her mom not to make her start a new school when the year was almost over, and her mom had given in. They'd had such a great time and taught each other so much that Malia's mom had agreed to homeschool her for fourth grade too.

Even though her parents hadn't said anything, Malia was afraid she might have to go back to regular school for fifth grade. Especially with a new baby in the way.

As Malia thought of the baby, her mom's belly gave a little jolt. "Your sister's kicking. Do you want to feel?" She guided Malia's fingers to the spot that had moved.

They waited. And waited. Just as Malia was about to give up and take her hand away, she felt it. Softer first, then a good solid kick.

Malia yelped and yanked her hand away. Of course, she'd known there was a baby growing inside her mom. She'd read the "Your Baby This Week" updates and memorized the developmental milestones. *The baby can blink and her eyesight is improving. All her organs are formed now; lungs and muscles are maturing rapidly.* But knowing there was somebody in there and feeling it were totally different things.

"Isn't it magical?" Malia's mom asked.

"I guess." Malia slid the blankets back over her mom's belly. "Magical" hadn't been the word in her mind.

"Your dad and I have been hoping for this miracle for years. I can't believe it's almost time."

Malia's heart dropped. All along, she'd secretly hoped the baby had been an accident, that her parents were making the best of a tricky situation. But maybe she'd never been enough for them. And now she never would be. She wanted to push away from her mom and clutch her closer, all at once.

"Are you ready for your birthday party?"

Malia shrugged, trying to pretend she hadn't just been hurt. "I guess."

"Did you invite any of your friends?"

"No. Just family this year." Malia had friends from the homeschool group, sort of, but none of them had called this summer. Having close friends—the kind who would like a big party with little cousins tugging at them, or the kind you could talk to when your mom was in the hospital—that was the thing she missed most about her old school.

Malia leaned against her mom and tucked the top of her head under her mom's chin. "It won't be the same without you."

Malia's mom sighed. "I wish I could be there, honey. But I got you something." She gave Malia a squeeze, then swung her legs over the edge of the bed. Malia jumped up to stop her.

"I'll get it. You're supposed to stay put. Your blood pressure is back up."

Malia's mom rolled her eyes. "My blood pressure is fine. And if I stay in this bed any more than I already do, I'm going to lose my mind." She shuffled carefully across the floor, rolling the IV stand behind her. From the back, she looked barely older than Malia, especially with her long brown braid reaching halfway to her waist and the pink hospital gown hanging nearly off her shoulder. Definitely too small to be growing a person inside her.

When Malia's mom turned around, she held a small blue box with a white ribbon tied in a perfect bow. "You can open it now or save it for the party."

"I'll open it now." At least one of Malia's parents had been ready for her birthday. She tugged on the ribbon with a little regret, knowing she'd never be able to tie the bow as perfectly as it was tied now.

When Malia opened the blue box, her chest tightened. There, resting on a bed of white satin, lay a silver necklace with a delicate harp pendant. The harp's neck curved gracefully, and tiny flowers had been engraved on the body. It even had impossibly small strings, like spider silk. Malia didn't dare touch them.

"The thing I miss most being in here," said Malia's mom, "is hearing you play."

Guilt pinched Malia's stomach. She hadn't taken her harp out of its case once in the last month.

"Thanks, Mom. It's really pretty."

Her mom took the necklace. "Turn around and lift up your hair, honey."

Malia obeyed. Even though she'd been putting on her own necklaces for years, it felt good to be babied just a little. She turned back to show her mom.

"It looks beautiful." Malia's mom held open her arms. "*You* look beautiful." Malia wrapped her arms around her mom's neck, partly because she wasn't sure how to put them around her waist anymore.

When her dad walked in, Malia and her mom were resting together, wrapped in a comfortable quiet. He laughed and shook his head. "You two sure know how to throw a party."

Malia smiled and let her eyes slip shut. She wanted to

save this moment of just her and her mom. Her dad spread a hospital blanket over them both, scratchy but warm. He turned the lights off, and Malia let her breathing match her mom's, slow and soft, until they were both asleep.

Malia

Chapter 6

MALIA'S REAL PARTY filled her house with laughter, presents, and sugar, just the way she usually liked it. But today, the laughter seemed too loud, the presents too bright and plastic, and all the food way too sweet.

Later that afternoon, when the guests were gone and the mess was mostly gone too, Malia needed some time to think. To be alone. Since it was her birthday, it didn't seem like too much to ask.

"Can I go to the church, Dad?"

Her dad looked up from the soapy sinkful of birthday cake plates. "I told your mom we'd stop by the library and find her something new to read, but we can do that tomorrow." He leaned over to check his watch where it waited on the counter while he washed the dishes. "Don't be too long, though. I want to spend some one-on-one time with the birthday girl."

Malia's church stood two blocks away on the side of a steep hill. It was really a cathedral, with stained glass windows and bell towers and even a few gargoyles. A tour guide had once told her that, compared with other cathedrals, it was very new and very small. But Malia couldn't imagine any place feeling older or bigger than the Cathedral of the Madeleine. It always seemed like the place where who she was and who she wanted to be matched the best.

Even though her family never went to church, the cathedral had been Malia's sanctuary ever since she'd first climbed hand-in-hand with her mom up its wide, gray steps. They had come to hear the children's choir sing, and

Malia had felt those voices wrap around her and rise to the vaulted ceiling.

Malia had truly fallen in love when one of the older girls had sat before them and woven music from the strings of her harp. Malia had gone home and made herself a small harp that very night from a cut-out cereal box and rubber bands. With a few repairs and improvements, the homemade harp had lasted until Christmas, when one perfect present had waited for Malia beside the tree.

Since that long-ago Christmas, Malia's mom had taught her to play the harp. They had figured it out together, really, from YouTube videos and careful attention to the performers at recitals.

"If business at the restaurant picks up," her mom would say, "maybe you can start taking lessons." Every day, Malia would practice until her fingers knew the notes and the notes turned to music. This summer, they'd finally scheduled a lesson with a real teacher, but they'd had to reschedule when her mom was hospitalized.

Now the rescheduled lesson was coming up soon, which was a big problem. Malia was too worried and distracted to practice even once while her mom was in the hospital. What if she wasn't any good anymore? She could ask her dad to cancel the lesson, but she had seen the lines in her mom's forehead, even today when they had both tried so hard to be happy. She couldn't add to those lines by letting her mom down.

Malia read the notice on the wide wood doors of the cathedral: *Concert tonight! Musicians may use this space to rehearse from 3-5 p.m.* Did she still dream of being one of those musicians someday? Malia wasn't sure anymore.

After she lit a candle and found a quiet spot near the front of the cathedral, Malia prayed. She had seen people praying and heard prayers on TV, so she knew exactly how to sit and what to whisper.

Please keep my mom safe.

Please keep the baby safe.

Please help me know how to be a big sister.

Then Malia thought the parts she would never say out loud, the parts she was ashamed to feel at all. *Please don't make me go back to regular school because of the baby.*

Please help me want to be a big sister.

Please don't let my parents love me less.

Malia's prayer was over, but she kept her eyes closed

and her head bowed. There were murmurs and shufflings around her, but she ignored them all. Until a soft sound began, and everything else around her grew still.

Malia opened her eyes and lifted her head. Someone was playing the harp. And suddenly, sharply, Malia missed playing the harp almost as much as she missed her mother.

Familiar notes filled the air inside the chapel. *I learned that last fall. Bach, I think.* Only it sounded nothing like the stiff notes she had played, the song she'd suffered through.

Then all at once, there was a voice too, singing in another language. Malia had never known there were words to this song. It was the most beautiful sound she had ever heard, like the music was sinking deep inside her. Without realizing it, she clutched and twisted her harp pendant, and the tiny silver strings did not break.

Malia added one last line to her prayer.

Please let my mom hear this song someday.

Later, when the sun had set and her dad was going over the books for the restaurant, Malia took her harp from its case. Then she tuned the strings, stretched her fingers toward them, and began to play.

☆

Before the restaurant opened the next morning, Malia and her dad went to the library. While he looked for the new books her mom had asked for, Malia dropped off the old ones, then headed straight for the row of computers with headphones attached. She wanted to find the song she'd heard in the cathedral, the Bach piece with the extra voice. Her version was called Prelude in C Major, but with a little searching, she found what she was looking for. With the extra part, the song was called "Ave Maria."

Malia scrolled through a long list of different arrangements: cello and violin, cello and piano, voice and piano, violin and harp. Finally, she saw it: harp and soprano. She fitted the headphones over her ears, closed her eyes, and bowed her head.

The music began, and it was just as beautiful as before. As Malia listened, two heavy tears slid down her cheeks. The song made her feel her mom's love somehow, but in an aching, longing way.

After the final notes, Malia looked up at the computer. She was about to click Play again when she felt a gentle tap on her shoulder.

Malia wiped her eyes and turned to see a thin old woman sitting next to her. "Did you need this computer?"

Malia asked, even though there were plenty of empty spots along the row. Maybe the old woman needed help using the computer. Malia's grandma could barely turn hers on without asking for help.

"Oh no, dear. I don't need the computer." Malia spotted a name badge around the old woman's neck—she must be a librarian here.

The librarian pointed at the song's description on the screen. "I just wondered whether you play the harp. Someone dropped a necklace by the book return just now, and I thought it might have been you."

Malia's fingers flew to the base of her neck, but there was nothing there. She'd caught herself touching and twisting the necklace ever since the cathedral, and she must have twisted too hard. She hadn't meant to break it. "Was it a silver harp pendant?"

The old librarian nodded. "It's lovely, dear. I put it in the lost and found. The children's librarians can show you where to find it, or I'll be down in a minute if you want to wait."

Malia thanked the old librarian and rushed downstairs for directions to the lost and found. The smaller drawers of the desk were almost empty, but the big bottom drawer was nearly full, and Malia's harp pendant sat right on top.

When she lifted the necklace from the drawer, the chain caught on something heavy. Malia followed it with her fingers to the very end, where the clasp had become tangled in the lock of an old leather book.

Malia set the book in her lap and began detangling the chain, grateful the clasp wasn't broken and had only come undone. She glanced at the book's cover, wondering whether it might be filled with music. The title—*Amicitia*—seemed Italian, and lots of music words were Italian. Malia definitely didn't need more music, but even after she freed her necklace, she wasn't ready to let go of the book. She'd never seen one with a lock before.

"Would you like to take it home?" The old librarian's voice surprised Malia, and so did the words she spoke next. "It's a box, really. There might be treasure inside."

A smile grew across Malia's face. "Yes, please." She'd needed something good to happen today.

The librarian handed the book to Malia. "Just bring it back soon and safe, and open it carefully. I know I can trust you just as much as the other two girls."

As her dad drove to the restaurant, Malia tried to imagine the other girls who had borrowed the box. She wondered if she knew them, wondered what treasure they'd found inside and whether it had been hard to bring it back.

When Malia set the box on the table of her favorite back-corner booth, a small paper star fell from it. She squinted to make out the words. THE ARROW IS THE KEY. On the other side of the star, Malia found a tiny ink drawing of an arrow and a key with an equals sign in the middle. She held the book up to the light and examined the arrow on its cover. All she needed was something small to pry the arrow out.

Malia grabbed a toothpick from the front counter and wedged it under the tip of the arrow. Seconds later, the book was unlocked.

The treasure turned out to be a thick postcard with a busy, bright painting on the front. Malia loved it right away. It reminded her of her family, partly because there were so many things happening at once. But then her eyes rested on the people at the center of the painting.

A mother and father pushed a stroller together. They made a perfect little family with exactly three people in it. Not four.

But was that really true? Everybody in the painting really did seem like family, not just the three people in the middle.

Malia looked above the stroller to where two girls jumped rope together. Maybe one of them was the sister. Maybe she wasn't being shut out. Maybe she was so happy with her friends that she didn't mind her family pushing the stroller around without her. Even if the girl's parents weren't right beside her, she wasn't exactly alone.

Malia wondered once again about the other girls who had borrowed the box, and whether one of them had left this painting just for her somehow. It felt a little like a puzzle to be solved. She definitely wanted to keep the painting, and the lines inscribed inside the treasure box told her it would be okay as long as she left a new treasure to take its place.

But she wanted to leave a different kind of treasure. Something comforting that might help another girl who felt alone and lost. Maybe even something to help a girl who was missing her mom.

Like "Ave Maria."

But how could she put the song in the treasure box?

She didn't have the sheet music for both parts, and probably the person who got it wouldn't be able to play the harp anyway. She could download it, but then what?

Malia remembered her dad's old computer and how he'd taught her to burn CDs on it before she got her iPod. That night, after a quick how-to reminder from her dad, Malia held a CD with the just-right song on it. She took a blue marker and wrote "Ave Maria" on the front, then added her signature symbol next to it—a butterfly whose almost-heart-shaped wings made the M and W of her initials.

Three days later, Malia took the box back to the library. When the librarian smiled and reached for it, Malia wanted to hold on a little longer. Her mom was still in the hospital. Her dad was still worried and a little overwhelmed. She still wasn't quite sure how to feel about her baby sister, and she was still afraid she might be sent back to school.

But Malia let the box go. She hoped someone would find her song and that it would make a difference to them. All she could do about any of it right now was hope, and the box had brought a little hope back to her heart.

Grace

Chapter 7

GRACE HAD CHECKED the lost and found every morning since she'd returned the box. But every day, she'd left disappointed. She'd kept the box five days, and now another five days had passed, so really, the box should be back. Hopefully it would have a treasure for her, one that would help her know what to do next. Grace wiped the dust from the rim of the bus window until every speck was gone. The box *had* to be back today.

When she reached the library, Grace hurried down the curved staircase. A cart edged its way around the corner of the chapter book section, and the old librarian soon followed. She brightened when she saw Grace. "Why, hello! I know you."

Grace meant to speak to Hazel. She tried. But she got caught between "Hello" and "I know you too" and "May I see the treasure box?" and her lungs and lips refused to form any of those words.

Even though Grace was almost always afraid of speaking, she was more afraid of not being able to. There had been months during third grade when the only adults Grace had said a word to were her parents and her teacher. Sometimes she had even worried that she would forget how to speak. But fourth grade had been so much better, and Katie had made all the difference.

And now Katie was gone.

If I don't fix this soon, it will only get harder. And then I'll never find a friend.

If the box isn't back, if the box doesn't help, it might be hopeless.

Grace chewed on her bottom lip, careful not to make it bleed. She didn't want anybody, even Hazel, to know how worried she really was.

The old librarian studied Grace. "Come with me, dear. I've got something for you."

Grace felt a seed of hope in her heart. Maybe the treasure box had come back! She pushed Hazel's empty cart to the storage room, then followed her to the small wooden desk.

As Hazel lowered herself into the chair, she caught Grace's eye. "Did I tell you that two more girls have borrowed the box already? The first one checked it out the very day you brought it back."

Grace dusted the edge of the desk with her finger. Had Hazel remembered to tell the girls "soon and safe"? Grace wished she could trust these unknown girls the way Hazel seemed to, but she just couldn't. People might promise they'd bring something back, or that you'd be best friends forever, but they couldn't always keep those promises. Even when they wanted to.

The librarian shuffled through the top drawer. Finally, she withdrew a small book covered in blue leather. Grace read the faded title embossed on the front cover: *My Little*

Book of Poems. Could it be another hollowed-out book box, with real treasure this time? Grace's fingers trembled as she opened the cover and looked inside.

But this book was full of pages, and every one was blank. Grace looked at Hazel and swallowed hard. There were no treasures here after all. No words inside for a girl who struggled to speak any of her own.

The librarian patted the empty space beside her on the chair. Luckily, it was a very big chair, and they were two very small people. The old woman held Grace's smooth hand in hers. "Don't be upset, honey. I thought you could write the words you can't say."

Now that they were together, snug and safe in the tucked-away room, Grace could finally speak up. "I can talk," she said. "You heard me before."

The old woman turned toward Grace. "Well, of course you can talk. But we all have words we can't say. And this book will be there, just waiting, until you're ready to say them." She smiled her kind, wrinkled smile. "Would you like me to write a poem in there to get you started?"

Grace nodded, and the librarian pulled a slim silver

pen from her bun. "Now, let's see," she said. "I think I can remember it all. Frost is one of my favorites."

Happiness bloomed inside Grace. Robert Frost was one of her favorites too, with his yellow woods and snowy evenings.

When Hazel had finished forming the words of the poem in delicate, shaky cursive, Grace gratefully accepted the book. Because a little of her courage was back, she asked, "May I check out the box again someday?"

"Of course, dear." The old woman smiled and slid open the bottom drawer. Grace's heart soared when she saw that the box was back after all. "You can take it today if you like. It's just as much yours as it is mine."

Back at home, Grace placed the box on her desk. Could there be treasure inside this time? It only took her a moment to open the lock and look inside.

Grace smiled when she saw the CD in its blue paper cover. She'd opened the box with an arrow, and now it had come back with a song, just like the title of her poem. It couldn't just be chance.

Even though it didn't seem like the right moment to

listen to the song, Grace wanted to be ready when the time came. She hurried downstairs to ask her dad's permission to borrow the CD player he kept in his study. Maybe she could even tell her parents about the treasure box.

But she didn't dare interrupt them. They were speaking in the quick, quiet voices that meant she wasn't supposed to hear.

"I've already withdrawn her from Edison and paid the deposit," said her mother. "And it wasn't a small deposit."

Grace's father made a coughing, choking sound. "You what?" he asked. "I thought we agreed that Edison is stronger in math and science. When did you start caring about the arts?"

"It's not the arts I care about," said Grace's mother. "It's the performance. She needs to believe in herself. She'll never get anywhere in life if she doesn't learn to speak up. She couldn't even answer the door for the delivery boy last week."

When Grace realized they were talking about her, she stepped into the kitchen. She couldn't help it.

Grace's mother glanced over and cleared her throat. "Oh, there you are, sweetheart! I have some wonderful news—I found a new school for you! I had to pull some strings, but you're on the list to start there this fall."

Grace imagined herself as a puppet with her mother pulling the strings. She struggled to swallow.

"Why do I need a new school?" Grace had thought she'd have one more year at her elementary school, where she was at least a little bit comfortable. Where she knew almost all the kids, even if they didn't know her.

"Don't worry, Grace. It'll be a new experience for everyone. It's a performing arts school!"

The fear tightened around Grace, cold and swift. She stared at her mother and repeated the words, unable to come up with any of her own.

"A performing arts school?"

"That's right. They're bringing in the very best people in music, theater, and dance. A performing arts school is *exactly* what you need to break out of your cocoon. You're ready to be a butterfly!"

Grace felt a little dizzy. "I'm fine in my cocoon."

Her mother laughed. "I know, sweetheart, but you'll be so much happier if you learn to get yourself out there! Think how it would feel to perform on a stage. To hear yourself play an instrument or sing a song in a huge auditorium, to see the crowd rise to their feet and applaud you!"

Which was exactly what Grace was already thinking about, and she couldn't imagine anything scarier. The perfect school for Grace would have quiet, comfy corners for reading and long tables where she could spread her stories and poems before her. Now that she thought about it, Grace realized her perfect school would be very much like the library. Definitely not a performing arts school.

Her mother was wrong about another thing too. Butterflies came from chrysalises. *Moths* came from cocoons. What would happen if Grace worked so hard to change and she turned out to be a plain old moth?

Grace's mother wrinkled her nose as if she were looking at a moth right then. "What happened to your shirt?"

Grace looked down. There was a dirty rectangle where she'd held the small blue book against her chest. "I wasn't careful enough. I'm sorry."

"Well, go change into something clean." Grace's mother checked her reflection in the microwave. "And bring that one down to me. I guess I'm doing laundry tonight."

Grace felt the weight of her fear pressing down on her shoulders as she returned to her room. A new school meant new routines and new kids and absolutely nothing familiar. It felt like a swirling storm had begun to gather, and Grace couldn't see a way out.

She dusted the blue book with a clean rag, wiping the surface vertically, then horizontally, again and again. Grace told herself to stop, that it was clean now, but another voice, the voice of her fear, whispered that it wasn't clean enough.

Her mother knocked, and Grace froze. Was she in trouble? Was there more bad news? Her mother's voice drifted through the door, thin and tired.

"I'm sorry I was so hard on you about getting your shirt dirty. And don't worry about the school. We'll figure something out. I promise. Can we talk?"

No. I can't talk. That's the problem. Grace couldn't move. She couldn't even cry.

After a long silence, a brochure and a packet of papers appeared under the door. "Just read through this and give it a chance?"

Then Grace heard her mother's phone ringing and the sound of fast footsteps walking away. She looked down and realized she was still gripping the little blue book, so hard her fingers ached when she uncurled them.

Maybe a poem can comfort me, like it did before.

Grace opened the book and read the title, written in the librarian's curly cursive. "Into My Own." She felt better for just a moment—until she read the poem.

Dark trees, mask of gloom, stretched away, edge of doom . . . it was terrible, and terribly frightening. Grace slammed the book shut. Even Robert Frost had changed. She picked up the brochure for the new school, but the forest on the back reminded her of the dark trees from the poem.

When a branch scraped across her window, Grace tore the page from the little book. She could never go to this school, and she had to tell her mother.

"Wait!" Grace slammed the awful poem and the brochure inside the treasure box, hoping they'd get a chance to talk about all of it. She clutched the box and ran into the hall before the loneliness and fear could swallow her whole. "Mom, wait!"

Grace's father met her at the bottom of the stairs. "What's the problem?"

"I need Mom. Where did she go?" Maybe Grace and her mother could fight the fear as a team, like they had before.

Grace's dad tried to hug her, but she dodged him and ran for the front door.

"She's gone," he said. "She got called to the hospital for a preemie." Grace's dad pulled her back inside. "What do you need?"

Grace wasn't sure why she couldn't tell her dad. She just couldn't. It was her mom who had helped her before when the doctors started calling the fear "anxiety" and telling Grace to take medicine. It was her mom who knew how to fix people who were sick, and Grace might be getting sick again. She spun around and started for the garage. "Dad, can you take me to the hospital to find her? Please?"

Grace's father glanced at the clock. "I guess. It'll give me an excuse to check back in at the lab." Grace waited while he shuffled through a pile of papers to find his keys, and then they were off.

When they pulled up, Grace pointed her father to the front doors instead of the parking lot. "You can just drop me off, Dad. I know where to go."

Grace's father gave her a worried, sideways look in the mirror. "Are you sure? You won't be able to see her until she's done anyway."

Grace nodded, and he turned his gaze back to the road. "Okay. I'll text her and let you know you're here. I'll tell her to meet you at the cafeteria. Keep your phone on you in case she can't come." As she swung the door open, he whispered, "I'm your parent too, you know."

"I know." Grace gave her dad's arm a squeeze. "And thanks."

Inside the hospital, the elevator tempted Grace to go upstairs and find her mother right away, but she couldn't disobey her dad. So instead, she let the escalator carry her to the cafeteria and settled in the back corner for what could be a very long wait.

Coming here had seemed like exactly the right thing to do, but why? Couldn't she have just waited? Or talked to her dad? The idea of a new school had scared her, but it was the poem that had pushed her over the edge. She opened the box and folded the brochure into a little envelope for the poem so she could feel like she was sending them both away. They definitely weren't treasures, though. She'd have to find something better before she took the box back to the library.

Grace looked up at one of the cafeteria's TV screens to check the time. After images of new equipment and smiling patients, a few words flashed onto the screen.

> **"Nothing in life is to be feared,**
>
> **it is only to be understood."**
>
> —*Marie Curie*

Grace forgot about the time for a moment and thought about the quote. It didn't sound right at all. What about sharks? What about tornadoes? It seemed like a good idea to be afraid of dangerous things.

Still, Grace found herself wanting the words to be true. Maybe if she read the poem again, if she really understood it, it wouldn't be so scary. Grace had just opened the box to give the poem another chance when a tray dropped to the table.

"Do you like cinnamon rolls?" A tall girl with round, brown eyes scraped back the chair across from Grace and sat down.

Grace nodded. "Mmmhmm." *It was almost a word*, she told her fear as she hid the box under her seat.

"Want to share?" the girl asked. "This thing is huge. Usually I share with my dad, but he wanted a little 'alone time' with my mom." The girl rolled her eyes and passed the bigger piece over to Grace. "She's a patient here. Is one of your parents a patient here?"

Grace had filled her mouth with a giant bite of cinnamon roll just in time. She shook her head. The brown-eyed girl guessed again. "Is one of them a doctor?" Grace nodded.

The girl played with her silver necklace, twisting it around and around. "That's awesome. Ever since my mom's been in the hospital, my dad says doctors have the most important job in the world. And my mom says it's the nurses. They think I could be a doctor someday."

The girl's cheeks turned so pink after she said this that Grace said, "You could!" before the fear could even try to stop her. "If you wanted to," she added, sinking a little lower in her chair. She popped another bite of warm, sweet cinnamon roll into her mouth.

"Thanks," said the girl. She let her necklace untwist, and Grace wondered if the silver shape on the end might be a harp. As the girl cut herself another bite, she asked, "What do you want to be when you grow up?"

Grace gave a smile and a shrug. She could answer that in one word. "Fearless." She pointed to the quote that had reappeared on the TV screens.

The girl laughed, and the sound of the laugh chased Grace's fear to the corners of the cafeteria. "I love that. When I'm a doctor, that'll be my motto." Her fingers found the necklace again. "Do you have any brothers or sisters?"

Grace shook her head. "No. But I used to hope my mom would have another baby. It seemed like a sister would be a built-in friend." The words slipped from Grace's mouth before she had time to be nervous. She'd imagined a sister for herself all her life—sometimes older, sometimes younger, but most often a twin.

"What if she was ten years younger?" the girl asked.

Grace had never imagined a gap that big, and she laughed in an easy way that surprised her. "Ten years younger might be trouble." She nodded at the next table, where a toddler was dumping out sugar packets while his mom talked on her phone.

When the girl turned and saw the sugar pile, she laughed too. "We should probably tell on him."

The boy ripped another packet open with his tiny fingers. Dimples dotted his cheeks as the sugar sprinkled like snow onto the chair beside him. "But look how happy he is," said Grace. "Let's help him fix it."

Grace folded up the edges of the girl's paper tray liner until it became a tray itself. She and the girl smiled at the boy. "Can I show you something?" the girl asked, and the boy nodded with wide eyes. His mom saw them and mouthed a thank-you, then turned away again with her phone.

The girl tipped the chair forward and Grace helped her brush the sugar onto the red paper tray. Then the two of them put the tray on the table in front of the boy.

"Watch this," whispered the girl. She used her fingernail to trace a shape into the sugar—a simple, beautiful butterfly. Grace leaned in and added a flower for the butterfly to rest on. The boy drew a squiggle next to it that could maybe be a caterpillar.

When the boy tapped his mother on the shoulder to show her, Grace noticed her tear-smudged eyes. The woman didn't want to ignore her son, but she definitely had something difficult to deal with right now. There really were so many things to be afraid of at the hospital, but so many things to be understood too. Just because your mom couldn't pay attention to you right then didn't mean she didn't love you.

After that, the little boy began writing *C*s in the sugar, and the girls returned to their table and their cinnamon roll. They talked about small things that felt important— the best foods in the cafeteria, the weird smell in the side stairwell, the best color of scrubs. (Definitely light blue, they agreed.) Grace was about to ask the girl her favorite song when she saw her mother coming toward her, lips tight and brow creased.

"Oh, sorry! That's my mom," Grace said, spearing one last bite of cinnamon roll onto her fork. "She might be in a hurry. Thanks for sharing!"

As she raced to meet her mom, Grace couldn't believe how easy it had been to talk to the girl once she got started. The rest of her fear floated out with one long breath. She snuck her arm around her mom's back and laid her head against the shoulder of her mom's scrubs. "Are you done already?"

"It was a false alarm, thank goodness. I feel like I've been going from one crisis to the next all day." Grace's mom stepped away and studied her face. "I'm glad to see you, Grace, but what's going on?"

"I was worried about something," Grace said, looking into her mother's tired eyes. "But we can talk about it another time. You should rest. I feel a lot better now."

Across the cafeteria, Grace could see the girl finishing her cinnamon roll with tiny white headphones in her ears and a hint of a smile on her face. Maybe Grace was getting braver—just a little bit, all on her own.

Grace and her mother walked together to the car and hummed softly to the radio all the way home. They said good night in tired voices outside their bedroom doors.

In the pale light from her window, the poetry notebook and treasure CD waited for Grace. Even though the moment still didn't feel right, and she didn't have a way to listen to it yet anyway, Grace pulled the CD from its blue paper case once again.

"Ave Maria." Grace had never heard of the song, but hadn't she just seen that butterfly somewhere? Rainbows winked off the surface of the CD, and Grace's heart fluttered as she realized that the butterfly before her eyes was exactly like the one she'd seen traced in sugar tonight.

Could this be from her? Did she have the box before me? It seemed almost too perfect to be true.

Then Grace sank to her bed with a sick shock of realization.

She'd probably never see the girl again since they hadn't thought to trade phone numbers or even names.

And if that wasn't bad enough, she'd left the box behind.

Jada

Chapter 8

JADA EXAMINED HER painting from every possible angle (including upside down) and still couldn't find a single brushstroke she wanted to change. That could only mean one thing.

It was finished.

Jada pushed back all the living room curtains and took down *Brownstones* from its place of honor over the couch. She hung her painting on the now-empty nail, then straightened it and stepped back to make sure her masterpiece looked just right.

A wide oak stood in the center of the canvas, made from broad strokes of brown. The oak's gnarled branches, exactly the color of Jada's arms, reached toward a sky heavy with clouds. Instead of a lush, green meadow, the oak grew from a field of salt. For this part, Jada had raided the kitchen cupboard and the bucket of rock salt the landlord had left in the garage. A serious coat of spray adhesive had gotten the salt to stick, but barely. Anytime she moved or touched the canvas, a sprinkle of white fell from it.

But the heart of the painting, the best part of all, was the tiny arrow sticking out of the canvas. Jada had used her dad's pliers and the scraps of copper wire to make the arrow. She'd pushed it through, right where the trunk of the mighty oak began to branch out. And from that very same spot, she'd dripped a thick line of blood-colored paint.

For the first time, Jada knew she'd painted something people would talk about and remember. Something that would make them *feel*. She couldn't wait to take a picture and send it to Grandma J and her old art teacher. They'd recognize her genius for sure.

Her dad was another story. Jada wasn't sure what to expect when she led Patrick into the living room and pulled off his dish towel blindfold.

"It's so . . . vivid." Patrick tugged at the collar of his shirt. "Sweetheart, are you okay? Is there anything you want to talk about?"

Jada rolled her eyes. "I'm fine, Patrick." She already regretted showing him the painting. Her dad was a smart enough guy, but he didn't get art. And even though he tried, he didn't always get her either.

Patrick brightened into his I-have-a-plan face. "Why don't we bring it to the school today? Mel can take a look and give you some pointers."

Jada shook her head. "I don't need pointers. It's finished."

"Well then, let's take it so she can see how talented you are." He stepped forward to grab the canvas.

"No!" Jada shouted, throwing her body between Patrick and the painting. "You can't just grab it or the salt will fall off!"

Patrick put his hands in the air and backed away. "Okay, okay. You carry it. I was just trying to help." He checked the time on his phone. "But hurry. I should have been there by now."

Jada managed to get the painting to the school with just a sprinkling of salt lost along the way. At first, she loved the idea of showing the painting to Mel and proving how good she was. But as the hours dragged on in her dad's classroom, more and more doubts buzzed through Jada's brain.

What if Mel doesn't get it?

What if Mel doesn't like it?

What if she tells Patrick I'm seriously disturbed?

Patrick looked up from his computer and saw Jada staring at her painting again. "Now or never, kiddo. We've got to go in a few minutes."

Now or never, Jada.

Now, I guess.

Jada gathered her art and her courage and headed down the hall.

The studio door stood wide open, but Jada still knocked as she passed through the doorway. Mel's face popped out of a supply closet in the corner.

"Jada! Good to see you!" She disappeared again. "I'll be right out."

Mel wasn't kidding. Before Jada had time to back away, she had closed the closet door and crossed the room. "I'm finally starting to get everything organized in there." Her eyes lit up when she saw the back of Jada's canvas. "Have you brought work to show me?"

"It looks like you're busy," Jada said, turning toward the door and almost stabbing herself with the wire arrow. "I'll come back another time."

"I needed a break anyway," said Mel. "I've been in there all day. I'd love to see it, if you'll let me."

Jada gently propped the painting on a nearby easel, then stepped back. She heard Mel walk closer and whistle, long and low. "That's incredible, Jada. What do you call it?"

"*Salt in My Wound.*" Jada was almost as proud of the title as the painting itself.

Mel reached toward the canvas, then stopped herself. "May I?"

Jada shifted in her shoes. "Okay, I guess."

Mel softly touched the arrow, then the salt. A few grains fell to the floor.

"Would you like me to spray some fixative on it? I'll

cover the painted parts first so it doesn't dull the color."

Jada was torn—keep her distance, or keep her master-piece in one piece? "Yeah, okay."

Mel finally looked away from the painting. "Your mom must be so proud of you."

Something tight and hard formed in Jada's chest. "Yeah. Right. She's so proud of me she doesn't even know what to say." Did everybody here have to bring up her mom? Jada bulldogged her jaw out and stepped away—straight into Patrick.

Patrick caught Jada by the shoulders and glanced from her to Mel. "Everything okay?"

Jada wiggled out of his grip and turned toward the door. "Sorry, Mel," she said, even though it was Mel who should be sorry. "We've got to go."

Jada grabbed her dad's wrist and led him down the hall. She marched to the parking lot and climbed into the passenger seat of the little Toyota, slamming the door. Patrick put the key in the ignition, then hesitated. "What's going on? Didn't she like it?"

It took Jada a second to realize he was talking about the painting. When she thought about Mel touching her masterpiece, Jada felt fiery inside all over again.

"Jada?" Patrick asked. "What did she say about your painting?"

"She loved it." *And if Mel loves it, it must not be any good.*

"So what was that all about?"

"Don't ask." Jada slumped in her seat and zipped her lips as she pulled out a Sharpie. As they drove, she drew the bold, thick lines of the tree and the piercing arrow on the cover of her sketchbook so she'd still have the image with her. When her dad eased the car over the cracks in their driveway, Jada finally spoke up. "Is she ever coming back?"

Patrick raised his eyebrows. "Mel? She'll be there all year, whether you like it or not."

Jada picked at the stitching on her seat. "Not Mel. Mom."

Patrick sighed. "Is that what this is about?"

"Yes."

"Do we have to talk about it? Again?"

"Yes." Jada didn't look at her dad, but she wasn't going to back down.

Patrick turned off the car and faced Jada. "I don't know if she's coming back, but I'd guess she's not. Especially not here."

"We could call her. We could ask."

Patrick shook his head. "One thing I do know about your mom is the harder you try to hold on, the faster she'll run away. If she ever comes back, it'll be because she chose it."

Jada nodded, but deep down, she disagreed. How would her mom even know how to find her, or how much she needed her? What if she really would be proud of Jada and all she'd become, she just needed somebody to tell her?

Jada wasn't so sure anymore that the treasure box could grant wishes. She'd put *Brownstones* inside four days ago, and she was still as stuck in Utah as ever. She looked up and down her street, at the row of houses and the kids jump roping and the sweaty mom pushing a stroller.

Aw, shoot. Shootshootshoot.

What if the box really works, but I put in the wrong picture and this *is my wish come true?*

Except for the space between the houses and the paint colors you'd use for the people, Emerson Avenue looked a lot like *Brownstones*.

Jada had to get her hands on that box again and find the right picture to put inside, just in case. But she couldn't think of any painting that would be the perfect fit.

A flicker of a memory flashed in Jada's mind. Who

was the artist the old librarian had recommended? Croquette? Cassette?

"Cassatt." After a few misspellings on her dad's old laptop, Jada typed the name correctly and found that Cassatt wasn't a "he" after all, unless boys could be named Mary. When she clicked on Images, the screen was tiled with paintings. Beautiful paintings.

Of mothers and babies.

Jada scrolled through dozens of them, and her artist brain took over enough to be impressed by the technique and compositions. Most of the paintings grew fuzzier and somehow flatter around the edges, like all the details had gathered in the center. It was almost like Cassatt was telling her, "Look here instead. This is what's important."

What was important in Cassatt's paintings were the people. They weren't perfectly posed or wearing their fanciest clothes. They were regular-looking people leaning over the side of a boat to look at a duck, or snuggled up in bed, or reading a book on a park bench.

Sometimes the people looked at each other, and sometimes they faced the same direction, like they wanted to see the same things. In one painting that looked kind of familiar, a mother washed a little girl's feet.

The librarian really had known what Jada needed. How else could she have suggested the perfect artist? It was Jada who had gotten the treasure-wish part wrong when she'd put *Brownstones* in the box instead of Cassatt.

But maybe wishing alone wasn't enough anyway. Maybe wishes didn't come true unless you worked for them too.

Tomorrow Jada would find the book box and print off her real wish picture—a Cassatt—to put inside. She'd check out some books on painting and famous artists. She'd teach herself since there wasn't a decent art teacher around. She and Patrick would start fixing up this falling-apart house so it would look like someplace a real family would live, at least until she could convince her dad to move back to New York.

Most important of all, tomorrow Jada would begin the official search for her mom. She couldn't survive this aching, out-of-place loneliness much longer.

Malia

Chapter 9

MALIA SLIPPED ON her headphones and found "Ave Maria" on her iPod as she watched the red-haired girl walk toward her mom. The music settled her thumping heart, but Malia kept replaying the last half hour in her mind. She'd just given half her cinnamon roll to a random stranger, and the stranger had turned out to be kind of awesome.

It had been a long time since Malia had shared a secret and a laugh with a friend her own age, like they did when that kid made the sugar mess. It had been even longer since anybody had just *listened* to her like the girl had. Somehow Malia had told her more about herself—about her *real* self—than she'd ever told any of her friends.

Except she hadn't told the truth about one thing. It wasn't Malia's parents' dream for her to be a doctor. It was hers. Malia didn't think her parents even knew.

But ever since she'd been coming to the hospital, she'd imagined herself wearing scrubs and maybe even a stethoscope, leaving at the end of long days knowing she'd made a difference. When families were scared and sick, she wanted to be the one who gave them hope. She'd be the kind of doctor who listened to people's hearts—or the tiny heartbeats inside them—and knew what to do.

If that girl thinks I could be a doctor, maybe I really could. It had felt good to say the words out loud.

When Malia's dad finally showed up at the cafeteria, she stacked her trash and got up to leave. The whiskered man at the next table touched her elbow and nodded down past Malia's feet. "Don't forget your book."

As Malia tossed her trash in the can, she almost argued. "Oh, thanks, but I didn't bring . . ."

And then she saw it—the leather-bound book box with the brassy arrow.

"Oh, right. Thank you." Malia blinked. "That *is* my book, sort of." Had the red-haired girl left it there? Malia picked it up and held it close as she headed upstairs with her dad, feeling like the box was an even greater treasure than before if it was connected to the girl.

When she reached her mom's room, Malia started her checkup right away. Blood pressure better, still no swelling, but something seemed different. Off, somehow.

"Did you have an ultrasound today?"

Malia's mom nodded. "Everything looks great. Now, tell me what's new with you."

Opening up to her mom seemed a lot easier after talking so much in the cafeteria. All Malia's stories came spilling out, beginning with the treasure box and the girl with hair as bright as a monarch butterfly. Malia almost opened the box right then, but her mom placed her hand over Malia's.

"You can save it for tonight, if you want," she said. "I

know there's not much anymore that's just for you. I want to hear about your harp lesson and your new teacher!"

"Her name is Miss Rousseau," Malia said as she straightened and stacked the mess on her mom's tray. "Dad says she's from France, but she looks like she's straight from a magazine. She said we've been doing a couple of things wrong with my hand position, but I'm doing almost everything else right." Malia stopped stacking and dropped her hands to her sides. "She says I have a gift." Malia bowed her head, but she smiled too.

"Oh, that's wonderful," her mom said. "She'll be able to teach you so much more than I could. Now you'll really take flight!"

Malia imagined all the beautiful songs she could learn, all the tricky fingerings that wouldn't seem so tricky with Miss Rousseau's help. Even in one lesson, she'd felt the difference a real teacher could make. She pictured herself playing in a grand concert hall with her proud parents in the front row.

But then Malia remembered the price Miss Rousseau had told her dad, and how he'd scratched his fingers through his hair and tried to figure out a way to say yes when they both knew the answer had to be no. Her mom wore that same worried look right now.

"It's not going to work, is it?" Malia asked. "It's too expensive."

Malia's mom looked up at the ceiling. "There's got to be a way." Which was almost exactly what Miss Rousseau had said. "We could save on payroll if I work some shifts at the restaurant."

"No, Mom. You'll be busy enough with the baby." *And with me.*

Malia's mom leaned back against her pillows. "You're probably right. But we have to think of something." She closed her eyes and drew her lips into a tight line.

The silence stretched out between them, and Malia could see the pain in her mom's face. She hadn't expected her mom to get so upset. Time to change the subject.

"Oh, by the way, I have a new favorite song! I heard it in the cathedral on my birthday. It's my Bach piece from last year, but a duet. With a voice."

The pain passed from Malia's mom's face, and she smiled. "I know that song—it's called 'Ave Maria.' You've heard it before too." Malia started to disagree, but her mom kept going. "You were little, though. It was the very first concert we went to at the cathedral. Remember when you came home and made that rubber-band harp?"

Malia's mouth fell open. "That was the song?"

Her mom nodded. "That was the song. I'm so glad you got to hear it again." Malia waited while her mom let out a long, careful breath. "'Ave Maria' really is amazing—not just the piece, but the history too. Did you know it was composed by two different people?"

Malia rested her chin on the foot rail of her mom's bed. "What do you mean?"

"Well, Bach composed the part you played. And then, over a hundred years later, a French composer added to it. He wrote a melody to fit an ancient prayer to Bach's prelude. I love the Bach piece. It's so beautiful by itself. But don't you think it's even more beautiful with both?"

Malia had to agree. "I'm going to learn it again, I think. But I don't know who would sing with me. Could you?"

A gentle laugh filled the space between them. Malia adored the sound of her mother's laugh, and she realized how much she'd missed it. "I couldn't do it justice. But thank you for believing I could. You'll find someone else to sing it with you, as beautifully as you deserve."

Suddenly, Malia's mom gripped the blankets and gritted her teeth. Malia sat straight up.

"Mom, are you okay?"

Her mom closed her eyes and let out a ragged breath. "Malia, can you get your dad?" Her fingers fumbled, then found the button to call the nurse.

Malia jumped from the rocking chair and began calling for her dad. After only a few seconds, he rushed in, and Malia hovered in the doorway, afraid they'd kick her out if she came closer.

". . . only the last few minutes, but they're getting stronger, so much faster than with Malia . . ." Her mom's voice disappeared into a tight, strained sound.

Malia's dad looked toward the door and seemed surprised to see Malia there. "Here," he said, tossing her his phone. "Call Kiana and tell her you need a ride home. I'm going to track down a nurse." He took two giant strides down the hall, then turned back to Malia. "Everything's going to be fine," he said. But he didn't look like he believed it.

Malia called Kiana—the youngest, most fun auntie in the family, and the only one without kids of her own. But Malia didn't want to get sent home, even with Kiana. She wanted to stay and help, to time the contractions and talk to the nurses. Or just to hold her mom's hand and be the one to say, "I'll be right here. I won't ever leave you." She was already kicking herself for not realizing her mom was in labor.

But a few minutes later, Malia was shepherded down to the front doors after barely a kiss for her mom. She clutched the treasure box to her chest and watched for Kiana's car in the looming darkness. Kiana let Malia sit in the front seat, but Malia almost wished she hadn't. Through the windshield, Malia saw the trees stretching their dark limbs toward the little car, and even her own street didn't seem safe.

Kiana tried to distract Malia with TV and buttery popcorn as they waited for her dad to call. But it didn't work, and he didn't call. Eventually, Kiana insisted that it was time for them both to go to sleep. After tucking Malia in, Kiana sat on the edge of the bed.

"You may be a big sister by morning," she said, smoothing the stray hairs from Malia's forehead.

Malia nodded. She had been preparing for this since spring. But she'd read enough pregnancy articles to know that delivering this early and this suddenly was dangerous—not just for the baby, but for her mom too.

"Kiana, is she going to be okay?"

"She'll be tiny, but those doctors know what they're doing. They've delivered babies even smaller than your sister, and those babies grow up just fine."

Malia swallowed. "I mean my mom. Is she going to be okay?"

Kiana bent over and planted a kiss on Malia's forehead. "Your mama is so tough. She'll be trying to take care of the rest of us by next week."

As soon as Kiana's light went out that night, Malia grabbed her iPod and snuck to her parents' room. With barely a sound, she slid between the still-straight covers of her mom's side of the bed. She tried to smell some trace of her mom on the pillow, or remember the way she looked when Malia came to wake her up on Christmas mornings.

But it wasn't working. Her mom still seemed so far away. Malia clicked on the bedside lamp. And there, half hidden under the lamp, was a flyer for the symphony last week.

The Salt Lake Philharmonic

——————— *presents* ———————

Dvořák's

NEW WORLD SYMPHONY

There was a sticky note on the flyer with a reminder in her mom's handwriting: "Buy tickets for M's birthday." Malia checked her iPod. Sure enough, her mom had put *New World Symphony* on it so Malia could listen to it and love it before they went to the concert. Her mom had done lots of stuff like that before she went to the hospital.

Malia pushed Play and closed her eyes. The first movement was sort of strange and a little scary, but the second movement was so, so beautiful. When it had faded out with one last peaceful chord, Malia snuck back to her own room with the symphony flyer tight in her hand. She slipped between her own cool sheets, wishing her new world were as peaceful as the one she'd just heard.

But the wind had begun to howl outside, and for the rest of the night, Malia's thoughts ricocheted between her mom's pained face and the too-small baby and her own uncertain future. The longer she lay in there, alone, the more Malia realized how much she didn't know about her new world. And how much it scared her.

Grace

Chapter 10

GRACE WOKE TO the sound of her mother's footsteps coming down the hall and straight into her room. A sick feeling gnawed at her belly, but in the fog of just-woke-up, she couldn't quite remember why.

"I have to go to work now, Grace. If you want to come with me again, you'd better hurry." She smoothed the quilt and studied Grace. "It's not like you to sleep so long. I feel like there's something you're not telling me."

Then all the worries that had kept Grace up late the last two nights flooded into her mind.

The fear was back. Not all the time like before, but it prickled and scratched at her a little more each day.

The treasure box was still lost. That memory was bittersweet, because Grace knew she'd only forgotten about the box because she'd met the cinnamon roll girl.

Grace had gone with her mother to the hospital the next day. But she hadn't found the box, and she hadn't seen the girl. She'd searched the whole cafeteria and scanned the faces of all the kids her age. She'd even scoured the dark, dirty closet that was the hospital's lost and found. Grace had hoped for the right moment to tell her mother about all of it, but her mother always seemed so tired or busy or both, and Grace never knew where to start.

Maybe I can tell her now.

But Grace's mother was already on the move. She straightened the basket of clean laundry on Grace's desk. "Well, even if you're staying here today, don't sleep any more now, or you won't be able to sleep tonight." She paused in the doorway. "Have you read the welcome packet from your new school?"

Grace picked at her quilt. "I took a look at the brochure." *Took a look at it, then folded it up and locked it away.*

Her mother let out an impatient huff. "Well, you'll need to look at the rest of it, especially the schedule. Unless you want me to pick your classes for you."

Grace shook her head. "No, I can do it. I'll do it today." Her mother would probably pick only classes with "performance" in the title.

She'd look at the schedule later, though. Today she'd fight the fear by visiting the library and spending some time in the sunshine. She grabbed a small blanket and headed for the bus stop.

When Grace got to the library, she decided to go to the garden first. The sky was so beautiful and the leaves were so green, and it couldn't hurt to give the box a little more time to find its way back.

Grace rounded the corner of the library, hoping to have the garden all to herself. She hesitated when she saw a girl with smooth brown skin and rows of tiny black braids sitting against the planter wall with a small sketchbook in her lap. Grace wished she dared wear clothes so bright or jewelry so colorful. This girl was definitely a butterfly, not a moth.

If only I had a cinnamon roll to share. Or something to say.

Grace waited a few seconds for the girl to notice her, then gave up and spread her blanket under a tree. She lay on her belly and propped herself up on her elbows, hoping that here in the fresh air and sunshine she'd finally be able to write a poem worthy of the blue book.

Over the next half hour, Grace's pencil scribbled and erased, pushed forward and paused, until she had the first stanza of her poem. She even had a title for it: "Friendship Lost and Friendship Found."

As Grace worked, she realized that the girl with the braids had turned toward her and was watching her with a slight frown. Grace glanced around at the bright flowers and the branches of the beautiful tree. The girl must have been drawing the garden, and now Grace had come in and messed it up.

Grace let her chest sink to the ground and hid her face in the crook of her elbow. She heard a sigh from across the garden and raised her head just enough to peek over her arm.

The girl had propped her sketchbook against the

concrete wall and was stretching her arms. She stood and began to shake her leg out. When she stepped to shake the other leg, Grace could see her satchel and her paper clearly.

The satchel had a logo on it exactly like the one on the welcome packet she'd avoided reading just that morning. It showed the silhouette of one straight, strong pine with the words "Learning Lasts a Lifetime" in bold, clear letters encircling the tree. Was this girl going to the new performing arts school? Would they see each other again, if Grace decided to go?

But even more than that, Grace's eyes were drawn to the sketchbook. The braided-hair girl wasn't drawing the tree or the blossoms anymore. The braided-hair girl was drawing *her*.

Grace was glad she could hide her face again with just a small turn of her head. She knew her cheeks would be bright pink. This had to be a sign the girl liked her, at least a little. And Grace hadn't had to say a word.

The image of the drawing stayed in Grace's mind. How had the girl drawn her so well so quickly? The trunk of the tree and slight folds of her blanket had only been suggested with a few rough lines, but from a distance, her legs and body and poetry book seemed almost perfect. Grace was sure it would look just like her when the girl finished the hands and face. She really wanted to see the drawing then, to know how the girl saw her.

Talk to her. This is your chance.

Grace knew that the longer she hid her face, the weirder she'd seem. Plus, she was making it harder for the girl to get back to drawing. But Grace couldn't think of the right thing to say. *Thanks for drawing me* wouldn't work. What if she wasn't supposed to see the picture? And she couldn't say *I think we're going to the same school* when she wasn't sure yet. Still, she had to say something.

Grace took a deep breath and stirred. She was about to ask the girl if she wanted to get ice cream from the library coffee shop, but the girl spoke first.

"Um, hey. Would you mind lying there like you were? Just for a little longer?" The girl pulled at one of her braids. "And also, is it okay if I draw you?"

Grace nodded. "No problem."

This was better. This was perfect. They could spend more time together, and she might not have to say another word.

Grace propped herself back up on her elbows and tried

to angle her legs just like they had looked in the drawing. "Perfect," said the girl. Grace couldn't help but smile for a second, even though she hadn't been smiling in the picture. The girl picked up her sketchbook again. "Thanks."

For most of an hour, they both worked. They breathed the same sweet air from the blossoms of the butterfly bush and shared the shade of the grove of sycamores as they each tried to make something beautiful from their simple sheets of paper.

Whenever Grace's shoulders and elbows started to ache, she sat and stretched, and the girl stood to stretch too. But they never rested for long, and before she knew it, Grace had finished her poem. She wrote a second idea for a title, "Butterflies," at the top of the page.

As Grace drew a curvy-winged butterfly next to her new title, a man with kind eyes entered the garden. When he saw the girl, he slowed down and smiled. "Hey. I thought you might be here."

The girl shut her sketchbook as he sat down beside her, and Grace gulped in a big breath when she saw what the girl had drawn on the cover: a tree with an arrow through its heart, just like her first poem. Had this girl found it?

"Ready to go?" the man asked.

Not yet, Grace thought. *I have to ask her if she got the box. And if she's going to the new school.*

But Grace's words wouldn't come, and the girl began packing her pencils away. "I guess. As long as we're going home."

"Or what if we went out for lunch, just me and you?" he asked. He put his arm around the girl's shoulder, and she leaned in just a little. Was he the girl's father?

Grace wished her father were here too, but he wouldn't be back until flight 4720 returned from San Francisco at 9:14 pm, two whole days from now. She tried to remember the last time her father had come looking for her and put his arm around her. The last time they had gone to lunch, just the two of them. With a pinch of guilt, Grace remembered how he'd tried to help the night she'd gone to the hospital. But she had shut him out.

The girl and her father began to walk away, matching each other step for step. When they had almost disappeared around the corner, the girl turned back to Grace. "Hey, thanks. See you around?"

All Grace could do was smile and wave, but the girl's wave and warm smile in return told her it was enough for now. It seemed pretty likely that Grace really would see the braided-hair girl around, and hopefully the girl from the hospital too.

Grace stood and brushed the grass from her blanket, then pulled out her phone to check the time. She nearly dropped it, though, when she saw the alerts that lit the screen.

Four missed calls, all from her mother. And one text: *Where are you? Please come home ASAP.*

Grace grabbed her blanket and hurried home, fast as the bus and her flip-flops could carry her. She'd have to come back and check for the box later. When she reached her house and saw her mother's car in the driveway, Grace ran up the front steps, wondering whether something was terribly wrong.

"Is that you, Grace? We're in the kitchen."

We? Was her father here too?

Grace rushed into the kitchen, hoping her parents were okay. But it wasn't her father sitting at the table, sipping a glass of lemonade. Even before the woman turned around, Grace recognized the smell of too much hairspray and the long, slick nails that held the glass.

It was Aunt Mona.

Aunt Mona was actually Grace's great-aunt and the

only member of their extended family who lived in Utah. Grace had been to Aunt Mona's house once, when she was four years old. She had knocked over several horse figurines in a domino-effect accident and had not been invited back.

Grace's mom pulled her into a hug with one hand as she checked her messages with the other. "I tried to call you, honey. I'm so glad I got to see you before I left, but I'd better get to the airport."

Grace grabbed her mother's arm as panic filled her chest. What was happening? Her father wasn't back from San Francisco yet.

"You remembered I'm going to Boston this week?"

Grace shook her head. Her mother had said she'd make it work, hadn't she? Grace didn't even know her mother's flight plans. And being alone with Aunt Mona definitely did not work for Grace.

"Your dad will be back the day after tomorrow. He talked to you about this, right? How we couldn't change our travel plans, but we found you a babysitter?"

Grace stiffened. Maybe her parents had discussed it with each other, but no one had told her. She tried to shake her head, but her mother just held her even closer.

"I thought you knew. I thought that's why you'd been coming to work with me. I'm so sorry, Grace. But your dad will be home in two days. You'll be okay."

Aunt Mona pushed her chair back with a sickening scrape. "Doesn't she speak?"

"She's just a little shy. She'll be fine." Grace's mother kissed the top of her head as tears stung Grace's eyes. "You'll be *fine*, honey. I'll see you when I get back, okay?"

Grace shook her head and held tighter to her mother's waist. Why hadn't she talked to her mother when she'd had the chance? Grace's home was the one place she'd always been able to find her voice before, but the words wouldn't come now that Aunt Mona was here.

Grace's mother reached for her suitcase and tried to wriggle free. "Please, Grace. Dragging things out will just make this harder for both of us." She walked to the door, then looked back. "I love you. I'll call you when I land, okay?"

And then she was gone. Grace stood at the window and watched her mother's car until it turned the corner, and the moment it disappeared, she began waiting and wishing for it to come right back. She heard Aunt Mona calling her from the kitchen, commanding her to answer.

Grace tried to take long, slow breaths, but there wasn't enough oxygen anymore. She tried to sneak up to her bedroom, but Aunt Mona heard the creak and came for her.

"Ten years old and you still can't talk?" Aunt Mona shook her head. "Don't worry. We'll fix this." She pressed her lips together and started up the stairs after Grace.

Grace's mind screamed and strained, but her muscles refused to run. She didn't want to be fixed—she wanted to be safe. But she never would be with this stranger in her home. Aunt Mona turned Grace around and led her back down the stairs.

The fear roared inside Grace and echoed through the empty shell she felt inside.

Jada

Chapter 11

JADA SAT IN her dad's classroom and looked over the results of her mom search so far. Nine Sarah Malones in New York City, and she'd sent letters or emails to all of them. But in a city of eight million people, shouldn't there be more Sarah Malones? What if her mom had left for Hollywood by now, and Jada was looking on the wrong side of the country?

A search that big would need a computer that didn't freeze every thirty seconds. Jada shut the old laptop she shared with her dad and headed for Patrick's classroom computer. But he beat her to it.

"Hey, I was going to use that."

Patrick shook his head. "Sorry, kiddo. I've got to get these assignments set up."

Jada sighed and flopped down at a front-row desk. "What am I supposed to do, then?"

"I guess talking to Mel is out of the question."

Jada rolled her eyes. "Good guess."

"Why don't you go down to the library for a couple of hours? I'll pick you up when I'm done."

Jada sat up, wondering why she hadn't thought of it herself. "Patrick, you actually had a good idea!" If she went to the library, there would be rows of computers and zero Mels. Plus, maybe the treasure box would be back, and she could put her mom-finding Cassatt wish inside. *Maybe today's the day I stop being so alone in this place.* She loaded her sketchbook and pastel pencils into her satchel just in case she got sick of searching on the computer. "Don't take all day, okay?"

"Two hours. Three, tops." He stopped typing and

pulled something out of his desk—a stack of folded papers with a bright red rubber band around the middle. He tossed it at Jada, and she barely caught it. "Take those brochures with you, okay? We're supposed to 'increase community awareness' about our school this week."

Patrick turned back to his typing before Jada could ask what her payment would be, but he answered the question anyway with his eyes on the screen. "By the way, we're really making ice cream tonight."

After a long, sweaty walk to the library with the taste of strawberry-peach surprise tickling at her tongue, Jada found the old librarian. She handed over the brochures and watched as the librarian chose one from the middle of the stack and tucked it into her pocket. The rest went into a plastic display case near the desk.

"Is the treasure box back yet?" Jada asked.

The librarian shook her head. "Not yet." She patted the brochure in the pocket of her sweater. "But I'll put this treasure in the drawer to save its place."

Jada's disappointment about the box mixed with her curiosity about the librarian. How did she figure that brochure was a treasure? And if it was, how had she known which one to pick from the stack?

If there really was library magic going on, Jada had to take advantage of it. She found a computer and looked through all the directories she could think of for any Sarah Malones she might have missed. She searched for images or article mentions. But the only new Sarah Malone in this search was sixty years old and surrounded by cats.

So much for library magic. It was definitely time to take a break.

Jada unslung her bag from the chair and found her way back to the spot where she'd picnicked with her dad. Maybe there was something here to draw. If she could block everything in with her pastel pencils before the sun shifted too much, she could take it home and make a larger drawing later, with real pastels on textured paper.

Jada sat at the base of the concrete wall and began sketching the tree in front of her. The fluttering leaves made patterns of sun and shade on the grass below, but it wasn't enough to make a really good composition. Plus, her last painting had been of a tree. Okay, it had been a bleeding tree in a field of salt, but still, her fingers itched to try something different.

Then the Cassatt paintings appeared in Jada's mind. They were the reason she'd brought her pastel pencils in the first place. She wanted to see if she could tell people what was important by where she put the details.

But Cassatt didn't paint trees. Jada needed a person.

At that very moment, a girl walked into the garden and spread a blanket across the grass. The girl's tangerine hair fell around her shoulders as she settled herself on the blanket with a small blue book. She didn't seem to notice Jada at all.

Just change her clothes and put her hair in a fancy bun and she'd look like a real-life Cassatt.

A shiver snuck up Jada's neck. This perfect setup couldn't be a coincidence. Jada glanced around, expecting to see the library witch reading her mind, guiding them both with invisible strings. But Jada and the girl were the only ones in sight.

Jada soaked in the scene in front of her for a few more seconds, then reached for her pastel pencils. This girl was exactly what her composition needed. The trick was to draw her before she moved.

She quickly blocked in the girl's body and her blanket with a dark blue. Next, Jada went back over the figure, working from the darkest areas where the girl's belly met the blanket to the lightest where the sun shone on her hair.

But it didn't look right. When Cassatt used soft blues and purples in the shadows of people's faces, it looked natural and beautiful. When Jada used those colors, the girl looked like a clown.

Jada studied the little Cassatt she'd been keeping in her bag, then blotted the girl's face with her eraser—again—and gritted her teeth. She had to get it right this time.

But the girl had disappeared. She had given up her propped-elbow position and was lying facedown on her blanket. Jada sighed and leaned her sketchbook against the wall. She stretched and flexed her aching arms, then stood to give her backside a rest. She'd been so busy trying to capture the girl on paper she hadn't noticed how sore she'd become.

After a little more stretching, Jada's mind and her muscles were ready to get back to work. But the girl still lay with her face hidden against her arm. Had she fallen asleep? Jada worried that her drawing might be stuck with a faceless blob in the center, which might be even worse than the blue mess she had now. She had to at least try to get the girl back in position.

Jada cleared her throat. "Um, hey. Would you mind

lying there like you were? Just for a little longer?" Heat rose to Jada's cheeks as she realized she'd never even asked the girl's permission. "And also, is it okay if I draw you?"

The girl lifted her head and opened her mouth, and Jada thought for a second she might say something. What if she got mad that Jada had drawn her without asking? What if she walked away?

But the girl just nodded and said, "No problem." Then she positioned herself exactly the same as before.

Jada let out a sigh and reached for her sketchbook. "Perfect," she said, grabbing a peachy-yellow pencil to catch the highlights of the girl's hair. She'd get back to the face in a minute. The girl smiled, and Jada wondered whether the girl thought she wasn't allowed to talk. That was actually okay with Jada, for now. The less they talked, the better she could concentrate.

For almost an hour, Jada carefully rendered the girl's face—the arc from her chin to her neck, the faint freckles on her cheeks, the way her hair tucked behind her ear. Jada was tempted to just draw the hair like it had been before so she could avoid the tricky curves and folds of the ear. But the artist in her knew it would look better this way. The girl was a writer, but judging by the way she turned her head just a little each time a bird called nearby, she seemed to be a listener too.

After a while, Jada finally felt satisfied with the face—even the blues and purples of the chin and cheekbones. She had just positioned her pencil to refine the girl's hands when she heard her dad's voice.

"Hey. I thought you might be here."

Jada slapped her sketchbook shut. It was bad luck for anybody to see her artwork before it was finished. Especially Patrick.

He knew better than to try to look. "Ready to go?"

"I guess. As long as we're going home." Jada began packing up her art supplies. She'd captured the girl's face, and she could use the shape of her own hands to fill in the rest. The wind was starting to blow anyway, which wasn't so great for drawing.

Patrick slipped his arm around her shoulder, warm and strong. "Or what if we went out for lunch, just me and you?"

Jada knew he was trying to make up for ignoring her all week, and they probably couldn't afford to go to lunch. But she'd take it. She wasn't sure how much longer she could survive on peanut butter and honey sandwiches.

Patrick and Jada had nearly rounded the corner when she remembered the girl. She was still under the tree, pretending to read her book, but Jada could tell from her sneaky glances that she was watching them. Jada had used that look herself on Mel lately.

"Hey, thanks," Jada called to the girl. "See you around?"

The girl smiled and waved, then turned back to her book. Jada hoped she really would see the girl again, and not just to draw her. She liked having friends who didn't mind quiet, and she was pretty curious about what the girl had been writing in the little blue book.

Patrick led Jada up the street to a tiny restaurant with palm trees painted on the door. "I've heard great things about this place."

"From who?" Jada asked. "Mel?" Patrick's half smile was enough of an answer. "I've never even heard of Hawaiian food! What if they eat weird stuff?" Jada took a step back as Patrick opened the door, and a fabulous smell floated out—sweet and spicy, exotic and comforting, begging Jada to come inside.

"Okay," she said. "We'll try it."

Jada and Patrick parked themselves in the very back corner, and a college-aged girl with a flower in her hair came to take their order. Patrick looked over the menu. "What's your special?"

The girl checked the blackboard, but there were only smudges and traces of already-erased words. "Malia!" she called. "What's the special today?"

Jada was surprised when a girl about her age poked her head out of the kitchen to answer. "Sorry, Kiana. I'm not sure there is a special today." She blushed and pushed her hair over her shoulder. "But I'll figure out something for tomorrow."

Jada was impressed. Was that girl in charge of the world's best-smelling restaurant?

Patrick folded his menu. "That's okay. I'll have whatever it is that smells so good. We're celebrating today." He winked at Jada. What was this all about?

"Perfect," said the waitress. "And for you?"

Jada stacked her menu on Patrick's. "Same thing, please."

As soon as the waitress had disappeared into the kitchen, Jada leaned forward. "Well?"

"Well, what?" A smile snuck onto the corner of Patrick's mouth.

"Well, what are we celebrating? You got a new job back in New York?"

Patrick rolled his eyes. "Very funny. The real good news is—I'm done! My classroom, my lesson plans, my paperwork. I'm ready for school!" He scratched his chin. "The first two weeks, anyway. But that means we can spend the next few days working on the house."

Jada relaxed. This really was something to celebrate. At least she'd have a few days Mel-free, and maybe she'd finally make some progress in the search for her mom. She just wished she could work for it *and* wish for it. If only the treasure box would come back.

While her dad was in the bathroom, the girl from the kitchen brought their water glasses. She set the glasses down, then reached across Patrick's side and picked up something from the booth bench. "Sorry," she said. "I left my book here."

Jada's jaw dropped. It wasn't a book—it was the treasure box.

"Is that yours?"

"Sort of." The girl paused. "I was going to take it back to the library later. Is it yours?"

Jada laughed. "Sort of. I've been looking everywhere for that thing." She thought for a second. "Well, okay, not everywhere. Just at the library. Do you want me to take it back for you?"

The girl looked at the box for a second, then held it out to Jada. "It feels like you should, you know? It sort of found me at the hospital. And now it sort of found you here."

Jada wanted to ask the girl whether any of her wishes had come true, but maybe she couldn't. Maybe it was like star wishing or birthday-cake wishing, and you couldn't talk about it out loud. Still, they could at least talk about the treasures, right?

The girl must have been thinking the same thing. She smiled a little and asked, "Hey, do you want to . . ."

An alarm blared from the kitchen. The girl's panicked face made Jada wonder if something was seriously wrong, but she didn't have time to ask. After a quick, "Shoot! No!" the girl disappeared, and Jada was left feeling more alone than ever. Even the delicious smell had turned smoky.

The waitress popped her head out of the kitchen. "Just a super-sensitive alarm. Sorry about that. Everything's okay."

But Jada didn't agree. Nothing was working out the way it should. She'd let Patrick drag her away from the garden girl, and she hadn't gotten to talk to the restaurant girl.

At least she had the box now. Jada grabbed the small Cassatt from her bag and made her wish as she locked it inside. But as she snapped the arrow key back into place, Jada found herself thinking about the girls instead. For a second, it made her wonder if she was really wishing for her mom after all, or just wishing to not be so alone.

Patrick and Jada stopped at the home improvement store after lunch, which wasn't exactly a new thing since their house was falling apart in a dozen different ways. But this time, he led her to the paint section.

For the first time, Jada felt a spark of creativity when she thought of the sugar house. She imagined covering the dirty, chipped-out walls with wide, smooth swaths of color, bright enough to match *Brownstones* or Grandma J's house. Colorful enough to remind Jada where she came from every time she walked through the door. But then Patrick took her by the shoulders and guided to her a hundred shades of almost-white.

"Um, no." Jada veered over to some nice, soothing blues. "What about this for your bedroom?"

Patrick guided Jada by the shoulders back to the boring section. "I'm thinking we stick with the classics. Which one of these would look best?" He cleared his throat. "For the whole house."

"Seriously?" Jada asked. They had never lived in a place where everything was the same color.

"Seriously. We just need one."

Being an artist, Jada could see that the samples were all slightly different. But none of them were anywhere near what she had in mind.

"Please, Patrick. I haven't asked for anything since we got here, but *please* don't make me pick from this section. I can't live in a house where all the walls are any of these colors." Jada covered her eyes. "What am I saying? Those aren't even colors!"

"Perfect for our Sugar House theme, right?" Patrick smiled and nudged her with his elbow, but Jada stepped away. She'd left behind and lost too many pieces of herself in the last few weeks. Suddenly, she couldn't stand to lose one more.

"It's not funny. None of this is funny! Moving me somewhere I'll *never* fit in, I'll *never* have friends, and I can't even pick what color the walls are?"

Patrick threw up his hands. "The landlord suggested cream. What am I supposed to do?"

"You're supposed to fight," Jada said, trying to keep her voice steady. "You're supposed to think about what I want. Who cares if the landlord *suggested* cream? What are you trying to do, drown me in cream? Every single thing is cream around here!"

The other people in the paint section had begun to look away. Patrick reached around Jada and pulled her closer, but she kept her arms stiff at her sides.

"I care, Jada. I do," he said. "There's good news and bad news for you, and they're both the same thing: We're not going anywhere for a long time."

Jada pretended to study the paint samples while her dad continued. "That's bad news if you really do hate it here. But it's good news too, because I think you're right. If you're going to live here a long time, I really do want it to feel like home. We can always paint it again later. Go ahead and pick the colors you want."

Jada nodded. She may have won the battle, but she'd lost the war.

Still, it was a pretty big battle. It felt good to talk Patrick out of boring beige and into daffodil yellow and new-leaf green. For her own room, Jada chose tangerine.

When they got home, Patrick and Jada lined up the buckets of paint along the wall in the living room. While he started taping off the trim, Jada headed to her room to change into clothes that already had paint on them. She figured she might as well take one more look at her garden girl sketch too.

But when Jada unloaded her satchel, something fell out she knew she hadn't put there—a small, sealed envelope.

Her wish couldn't be coming true already, could it? Jada snatched it up and slid her finger under the flap, pulling out the small scrap of paper inside.

I think it's time for you to have this. I think your mom's as ready as she'll ever be.
Good luck . . .

Sara Malone
saramalone326@gmail.com

Jada sucked in a deep breath. No wonder her searches hadn't worked—her mom had changed the spelling.

Why the H did she drop the H? Jada shook her head. She

didn't really care. All that mattered was that she'd finally found her mom.

Jada's pastel pencils stayed untouched in their box; the sketchbook lay open across her bed. She forgot all about the buckets of paint and the ice-cream maker. Without wasting even a heartbeat, Jada hurried to the computer and began to type.

Malia

Chapter 12

WHEN THE SUN streamed through Malia's window that morning, she knew she was waking up to a new world. She blinked the sleep from her eyes and read Kiana's note on her nightstand.

> The baby's small but healthy.
> You're a big sister!!

It took a minute for the message and all it meant to sink in.

It happened. I'm a big sister. And so far, everybody's okay.

So far, I'm okay.

The melody from the night before still echoed like a soothing soundtrack through Malia's mind, and when she looked a little closer at the concert flyer, she realized the melody was written as a decorative border across the bottom. She circled the line of music with a thick blue marker, then grabbed a piece of staff paper from her music basket to write out the first two measures for herself.

As Malia hummed the notes, Kiana leaned around the doorway.

"Hey! You're awake! Hurry and get ready. We've got to open the restaurant, and then we'll go meet your baby sister."

"Hang on," Malia said. "I'll be right down."

Malia pulled on a clean shirt and her favorite comfy shorts. Something inside her whispered that she should bring the box along, that she might want something old and familiar to hold on to. Maybe she could return it to the red-haired girl, if she saw her at the hospital again.

First, though, she'd need to put in a treasure of her own, and there wasn't much time. Malia's gaze fell on the melody on the symphony flyer. Sending a song in a new way felt just right.

When Malia opened the box to trade out her treasure, she found a little poem inside a homemade envelope. Malia traced the edges of the envelope with her fingers, wondering whether it had been folded by the same fingers that made the paper tray for the little boy at the hospital. Had this treasure really come from the red-haired girl?

"I'll be in the car!" Kiana called from downstairs.

Malia slipped the envelope and the poem into her nightstand to save for later. She took the symphony flyer with the melody on the bottom and locked it in the treasure box. Even if she didn't find the red-haired girl, she hoped it could help another girl trying to find her way in a new world.

When they got to the restaurant, Malia headed to her favorite booth at the back. She went over the to-do list her dad had left for her.

FILL THE SALT SHAKERS

WRITE THE SPECIAL ON THE CHALKBOARD

MAKE A NEW BATCH OF HULI-HULI SAUCE

If she worked through the list backward, the jobs would get easier as she went. Malia headed for the kitchen and began setting out ingredients on the slick steel counter. Honey, ginger, soy sauce, sesame oil . . . She mixed them in just the right ratios and stirred them on the stove. Soon Malia's favorite smell filled the kitchen.

Malia didn't know many words in Hawaiian, but she knew "huli" meant "turn," and that was how they made the chicken. Since she was very small, Malia had loved to watch her dad painting on the flavor with his big basting brush as the chicken turned on the rotisserie. He'd always cut off the first bite for her to taste. "What do you think?" he'd ask. "Should I huli some more?" Malia would nod, even though it tasted perfect, and he'd pick her up and spin her around.

Now he'll do that with the baby, too.

Kiana's voice pulled Malia back to the restaurant. "What's the special today?"

Malia poked her head out of the kitchen and saw a girl

her own age sitting at the back booth with her dad—just the two of them. She realized she had no clue what the special was supposed to be.

"Sorry, Kiana. I'm not sure there is a special today." Malia didn't think her dad's note had said what the special should be, but maybe she'd forgotten. If she'd done the list in order, she'd at least be working on the chalkboard by now. "I promise I'll figure out something for tomorrow."

Malia hustled back into the kitchen and filled the salt shakers. She rinsed a batch of rice and put it in the cooker, even though that wasn't on her list. She set the timer for the rice to simmer and gave the sauce a stir. Everything was going well, but something still bugged her in the back of her brain. Something about those customers in the back.

They're sitting in the back booth.

I left the box in the back booth.

Malia filled two water glasses and headed straight for the dining area. The girl's dad was gone, which made going over there way less intimidating. Relief flooded through her when she saw the box on the bench, untouched.

"Sorry," she said as she set the glasses down. "I left my book here." Malia rested one knee on the bench and reached across to grab the box. When she looked up, the girl was staring at her with her mouth hanging open. "Is that yours?"

"Sort of. I was going to take it back to the library later." *Unless I could find the red-haired girl first.* "Is it yours?"

"Sort of. I've been looking everywhere for that thing!" The girl scratched her arm. "Well, okay, not everywhere. Just at the library." She reached for the box just a little. "Do you want me to take it back for you?"

The look in the girl's eyes told Malia they both knew the secrets of the box. "It feels like you should, you know? It sort of found me at the hospital. And now it sort of found you here."

Malia handed the box to the girl, hoping they could sit down together and talk about where her treasures had come from, and where they'd gone. "Hey, do you want to . . ."

Just then, the smoke alarm blared. *The sauce!*

"Shoot! No!" Malia sprinted to the kitchen.

Blooms of black smoke curled from the saucepan. Malia slid one hand into an oven mitt and grabbed the handle, turning the burner off with the other. Kiana rushed in with a fire extinguisher, but the smoke was already floating away and the alarm had fallen silent.

Kiana let out a deep breath. "Everything's okay." They looked at each other and at the blackened mess. "Well, except the sauce. I'll go tell the customers it's nothing to worry about."

Before Kiana returned, one of the regular waitresses walked in. She tied her apron around her waist and clipped a fake hibiscus in her hair while she spoke to Malia at sixteenth-note speed.

"Wow, it smells like smoke in here. Where's Kiana? You guys can go now. I'll have the cooks finish up that rice. And wash that pan. Wow. I guess we still need more huli-huli sauce? Sorry I couldn't get here sooner. Say hi to Emily and the baby for me!"

By the time the waitress had finished talking, Kiana was back and had already grabbed her keys. "We will. Can you finish taking care of that dad and daughter too?"

Before she even got an answer, Kiana dragged Malia out the back and into the car. "I cannot wait another minute to see that baby! Buckle up, Malia. We might be driving kind of fast today."

Malia and Kiana arrived at the hospital in record time and raced up the windy walkway. Malia had barely caught her breath when the elevator doors dinged open and most of her family poured out. Right away, the cousins pulled at Malia and peppered her with news.

"We saw her, Malia! We saw your baby sister!"

"You have to look through the glass, like at the aquarium. You can't touch her." Malia had never seen Kai look so serious.

"The card says 'Baby Girl Wood.' That's not her real name, is it, Malia?"

They all saw my baby sister before I did.

Kiana gave Malia's hand a squeeze and pulled her from the rest of the relatives. Upstairs, they found Malia's dad, still wearing yesterday's clothes. Malia rushed to him and wrapped her arms around his waist. He planted a kiss on her forehead, then stepped out of her hug.

"Are you ready to see her? She can't wait to see you!" Malia's dad guided her down the hallway. They stopped in front of a glass door with big, bold letters across it: Neonatal Intensive Care Unit: Authorized Personnel Only.

"Stay here, guys. I'll bring her to the window." Malia's dad grinned, full of energy even though he had dark crescents under his eyes. "You're going to love her!"

Malia followed Kiana to a huge window and waited.

She didn't agree with Kai at all. This was nothing like the full, floating feeling of watching the aquarium, where life bloomed in every direction. Here, life was so fragile that even breathing could be dangerous, and even heartbeats had to be helped by machines sometimes.

After a few moments, Malia's dad appeared, grinning and waving as a nurse wheeled in a small cart with blinking monitors below a clear plastic case. But when were they going to bring the baby in?

Then Malia saw her, inside the plastic with just two hand-sized holes for anyone to reach her. She seemed even smaller than a sweet potato.

Malia didn't want to look at all the wires and tubes and needles connected to the baby, but there didn't seem to be anywhere else to look. She tried to remember her cousins when they were babies, and all the pictures in her mind showed round, happy faces, rounder tummies, and folds of fat on their legs. This baby had a round tummy, sort of, but her legs and arms were so, so skinny.

Were they sure this was the right one? Malia looked up to ask Kiana that very question, but when she saw tears tracing down Kiana's cheeks, she knew the answer.

Malia bowed her head, embarrassed that she hadn't

even recognized her own sister. She was officially the last one in the family to see the baby.

"What do you think?" When he spoke through the glass, Malia's dad sounded far away.

Malia nodded and smiled. "Wow. She's so tiny."

"Three pounds, eight ounces, and she'll probably get a little smaller before she gets bigger. The doctors hope she won't drop below three." Her dad barely glanced up from the baby.

Malia placed her hand against the glass. She'd read so much about preemies, but she still didn't feel like she knew anything at all about *this* baby. Mostly she just wanted to see her mom.

Kiana understood. She leaned over and whispered in Malia's ear. "Let's go find her, honey." Then she stood and spoke through the window. "We're going to see Emily, okay?"

Malia's dad glanced up and nodded. "I'll be in soon. Love you, baby girl." But by the time he'd finished speaking, he was already looking down again, so Malia wasn't even sure he was talking to her.

Kiana left Malia alone with her mom so they could have some privacy, but she shouldn't have worried about that. All Malia's mom wanted to talk about was the baby, and when Malia finally got a chance to talk about the symphony flyer and the girl from the restaurant, her mom couldn't keep her eyes open any longer.

Malia thought back to her birthday, when she and her mom had fallen asleep in the hospital bed next to each other. It seemed like so long ago, and Malia felt too old for stuff like that now. So many last things had happened lately—her last nap with her mom, her last day as an only child. Why didn't anybody ever warn her when she was doing something for the last time?

"What did you think? Isn't she amazing?"

Malia hadn't even heard her dad come in, and it took her a second to realize he was talking about the baby.

"She's amazing." And Malia meant it—the baby was amazingly tiny and had an amazing amount of attention focused on her. Would it be like that from now on? If Malia was a good enough daughter, a good enough sister, would her parents still love her like they had before? Or was that just something parents said, even though everybody knew it wasn't really true?

Malia's dad shook his head. "I still can't get over how small she is. I can almost circle my thumb and my middle finger around her belly. But she'll grow. She won't have that tube down her throat forever—just until she learns to nurse. And once she learns to do that, we can take her home!"

Malia wasn't sure what would happen to the rest of the tubes and wires, and she wasn't ready to think about the baby coming home yet. "Yeah, that's amazing too. Hey, speaking of home . . ."

Her dad's gaze drifted out the window, where the wind whipped the branches and stirred up swirls of dust on the sidewalk. "We probably should get out of here. The nurses say it's just going to get windier. We need to let your mom rest anyway. She was so busy staring at that baby she didn't sleep all night."

Malia blinked back tears as she and her dad made their way to the parking lot. Her mom hadn't slept all night because watching the baby lie there was too important, but when Malia showed up, she fell right asleep.

When they got to the car, Malia's dad tossed her his phone. "There's a voice mail on there that's probably for you," he said. "You listen and I'll drive. Unless you want to trade." He shot Malia a wink and turned the key.

Malia found the voice mail, and her stomach skipped

when she read the name: *Julia Rousseau*. She forgot about the baby for a minute and pressed Play, hoping the harp teacher had found a way for her to keep taking lessons.

"Hello, Wood family! I've found the perfect solution to both our problems. I've agreed to join the faculty at a new arts school called Evergreen Academy, and full-time students there have the option of private lessons during the school day. It almost reminds me of my music school in Paris! Anyway, I know what a strain Malia's homeschooling has become on your family, so we'd be solving that problem as well. I realize it's short notice, but there's just one last scholarship opening, and it may fill up fast. Please call me back right away!"

The skip in Malia's stomach turned to a sickening ache. Her parents really didn't want her around so much anymore, but it was even worse than that.

Malia knew what happened when kids went to special performing arts schools. Her friend Matthew from her old neighborhood had been so good at the piano that he'd gone off to a special school up by the university. After that, he'd spend an hour a day driving and three hours a day rehearsing and nobody really saw him much, including his family. This new school might be even worse and farther away.

Malia deleted the message and passed the phone back to her dad. "What did she say?" he asked.

"Nothing." Malia had never lied to her dad before, and she had to look out the window to make the words come out. "She doesn't have any ideas yet. I guess it might not work out after all."

"That's too bad," said Malia's dad as he flipped the turn signal. "By the way, I need your help with something. We can't keep calling your sister 'baby,' but we haven't found the right name. Nothing seems good enough. Can you try to think of a name for her?"

Malia yanked her hood over her head as they eased into the driveway so he wouldn't see the guilty look on her face. "Sure, Dad. I'll think about it." Then she stepped out into the wind so she wouldn't have to hear whatever wonderful thing he said about the baby next.

Grace

Chapter 13

AS THE BRANCHES scraped and scratched Grace's window, she worried about how much damage the wind might do today. She had hoped to visit the library to get away from Aunt Mona and check for the lost treasure box, but now Grace wasn't sure she could go out at all.

When Grace was younger and too afraid to watch *The Wizard of Oz*, her parents had told her there was no such thing as witches, and no such thing as tornadoes in Utah because of all the mountains.

But when her fourth grade class had studied Utah history, Grace had found out about the tornado that tore through Salt Lake when her parents were in college. One they must have conveniently forgotten about, even though it had started right in their neighborhood. If her parents hadn't told the truth about tornadoes, Grace couldn't be totally sure that witches didn't exist.

Speaking of witches . . .

Grace sucked in a breath as Aunt Mona's footsteps approached.

"Did you sleep well, Grace?"

Grace turned, eyes toward the floor. She nodded.

"You will look at me, and you will answer me. With actual words. I promise you, Grace, I'm only doing this to help. Now let's try again." Aunt Mona cleared her throat. "Did you sleep well, Grace?"

Grace looked up. She swallowed. But after a very long minute of trying to form even one word, Grace's face began to burn and she turned away. She wanted to answer, just so Aunt Mona would leave her alone.

But the words wouldn't come, and the truth wouldn't

have been the words Aunt Mona was looking for anyway. Grace hadn't slept at all. There had been Christmas Eves when she'd thought she'd stayed awake all night, but now Grace knew she'd been wrong. Now she knew what a whole night felt like—how long, how dark, how lonely. It had been even worse knowing that her parents were spread across the country as the wind rattled the window screens and haunted the chimney. Grace didn't think she could survive another night like that.

"Honestly, Grace," said Aunt Mona. "You cannot expect to make it in this world if you won't speak to people." Aunt Mona folded her arms and drummed one set of emergency-red fingernails against her sleeve.

Grace nodded again. *I have to survive. I have to get away from her.* She took her library card from her bag and held it out toward her aunt.

Aunt Mona waved the card away. "Yes, your mother told me you'd probably want to go to the library. But how are you going to find a book if you can't even ask the librarian for help with the card catalog?"

Grace wasn't sure what a card catalog was, but she felt a spark inside her that wouldn't let her give up. She gave the library card a little jerk and held it closer to Aunt Mona.

"You may go to the library when you ask me with actual words instead of this ridiculous game of charades. And not until then."

As Grace slipped her library card back into her bag, she felt the spark inside her grow into a small flame. Aunt Mona was horrible. Even though Grace didn't wish a house would land on top of anybody, she didn't think it would be so bad if the wind picked up her aunt and took her away.

Either that, or Grace would have to escape. She was more determined than ever to go to the library, wind or no wind. Her chance came as she cleared up Aunt Mona's lunch mess.

"I need to lie down," Mona said. "You'll be quiet, won't you?" Her lips curved into an awful smile. "Well, look who I'm talking to. Of course you will!" She cackled at her own joke as she closed the door to the guest bedroom.

When Grace was sure her wicked aunt was really resting, she tore a piece of paper from her notebook. In neat block letters she printed, "May I go to the library?" and placed it on the floor outside the guest bedroom. And since she'd already been told she could go to the library if she asked with real words—and she had—Grace slung her bag over her shoulder and stepped out into the storm.

The trek to the bus stop took twice as many steps as usual. Each time Grace lifted her foot to push it forward, the wind seemed to push it right back before it hit the sidewalk. Bus rides were always bumpy, but Grace had never felt the bus jerk and sway like this.

When the bus pulled up to the library, Grace jumped from her seat. She dashed down the steps and through the ferocious wind and didn't stop until she'd reached the very back corner of the reading attic, safe underground.

Grace hugged her knees and leaned her forehead against them. She took deep breaths, grateful that the air filled her lungs without thrashing against her body; grateful that, finally, everything around her stood silent and still.

After twenty-four deep breaths, Grace released her knees and stretched her legs. And then she saw the girl from the garden, carrying not her sketchbook, but a brown leather book.

Could it be the treasure box book? Grace snuck out of the reading attic and peeked around a row of shelves. The girl was handing something to the librarian, and Grace got goose bumps when she realized it was exactly what she'd hoped it would be. *Amicitia* had found its way back! It hadn't gotten lost at the hospital after all!

And maybe this meant something more. If the garden girl had checked out the friendship box, maybe she knew what it felt like to be lonely. Maybe she knew what it felt like to be left behind.

Grace begged her feet to carry her forward, begged her voice to speak. *I'm Grace, and I know about this box too. I'm the one who made the paper star and left the poems.* That's all it would take, and they'd be friends for sure.

But after the day she'd spent with Aunt Mona, Grace just couldn't make herself step forward or speak anymore. All she could do was watch and ache as the girl said something to the librarian and handed her the box, then rushed back upstairs.

Grace sat down and began to bite her thumbnail, telling herself again and again that she wouldn't cry. Then a gentle hand fell on her shoulder, and Grace looked up to see Hazel standing behind her.

The old librarian smiled. "I hoped that was you. Look!" She held out the box to Grace. "This just came back in. If only you'd been here a few minutes sooner, you could have met the girl who brought it back."

Grace nodded, unable to tell Hazel she'd been here soon enough, she just wasn't brave enough. The librarian set the box in Grace's lap. "Something tells me you'd like another turn." Grace nodded again, and the old librarian smiled. "Well, soon and safe, please. As you know. The three of you just keep taking turns, don't you?" She gave Grace one last knowing smile and was gone.

The three of us.

Me, the girl from the garden, and the cinnamon roll girl?

Grace couldn't be sure about the last one, but who else could it be? She took out her ponytail and began to divide her long hair into three equal parts. *The three of us,* she thought again, folding the thick sections of hair over and over in turn until she had a strong, straight braid down her back.

With the treasure box tucked inside her bag, Grace could face the wind again, and she might even be able to face Aunt Mona too. But just as she started up the stairs, Grace saw someone she wasn't prepared to face at all.

The girl from the garden was back already. She was coming down the stairs. She was headed straight for Grace.

When the girl saw Grace, her eyes widened. "Hey! Thanks again for letting me draw you. I'll have to show you when the big version's finished—it turned out pretty good."

Speak, Grace.

The fear prickled at Grace's skin, but she tried to fight it.

You have to say something. You have to.

Beads of sweat formed under her bangs.

Just one little sentence.

Even one little word.

Her hands began to shake, so she shoved them in her pockets.

You already lost one chance today. Say something!

As the seconds ticked by, the girl began playing with one of the braids at the back of her neck and glancing toward the computers. Then the moment passed quickly and so did the girl, with another "See you around!" thrown over her shoulder.

Grace brushed the sweat from her forehead and tried to steady her hands. There had to be another way to get her message across. She grabbed paper and a pencil to write the girl a note, but she wasn't even sure how to start it. She didn't know the girl's name or much about her at all, and she didn't dare just walk up to her and hand her a note anyway. Grace didn't want to seem even stranger than she already had.

Grace dropped her shoulders in defeat—until she saw a corner of brown leather peeking out from her bag. *Amicitia!* She'd use the treasure box! Instead of someone else's poem, she'd use her own this time. *Take this treasure, leave one of your own.* Maybe that's what she should have done all along.

Now, with a sure, steady hand, Grace printed the lines of the friendship poem she'd written in the garden next to the very girl she hoped would read them now. She thought of the brown-eyed girl from the hospital and changed the last stanza, just a little. Now her poem would find either the girl from the hospital or the girl from the garden. She took out the new treasure without looking at it—wanting to save this one too for the perfect moment—and slipped her poem inside the carved-out pages of the old book.

Hazel raised her eyebrows when Grace returned the box a few minutes later. "Well, I'd say this qualifies as soon," she said with a gentle laugh. "Come back and borrow it again, won't you? You can visit me too. Another kind of *amicitia*." Grace smiled and nodded. When she turned to leave, Hazel called after her. "Be careful in that storm!"

Once again, the wind rocked the bus and nearly blew

away Grace's bag. But she held tight, feeling that the time had almost come for both treasures she'd found in the box—today's slip of paper, and the CD from before. Grace had thought she'd been saving it for a special occasion, but maybe she'd been saving it for a Mona-sized emergency.

When she made it safely home, Grace snuck into her father's office, knowing she wasn't allowed, but also knowing her father's small CD player and headphones were in the cabinet behind his desk.

"Grace! Is that you?" Aunt Mona marched down the hall and threw the office door open as Grace slipped the CD player into her bag, her hands hidden by the cabinet door.

"Get out of here! This room is off-limits." Aunt Mona grabbed Grace's arm and forced her to stand, her long, slick fingernails digging into Grace's skin. "You know the rules, don't you? You just choose to ignore them. I saw your note. I know you disobeyed and went to the library."

The claws dug a little deeper as Aunt Mona dragged Grace from the room. Grace wanted to tell her aunt that she hadn't disobeyed, that she had wanted her aunt to see the note. But, of course, the words wouldn't come.

"Don't worry," said Aunt Mona. "Your mother may be

too busy or too weak to teach you proper manners, but I am not." She grabbed her car keys from the kitchen counter and shook them inches from Grace's face. "Grace, my dear, we're going out."

Chapter 14

JADA SAT CROSS-LEGGED on her bed with a blanket over her shoulders, amazed that her wish seemed to be coming true before she'd even finished wishing it. She tapped her pastel-stained fingertips on the side of the laptop as she read the message she'd typed. Even though she'd read it fourteen times already and had been working on it since the night before, there was always something little to change.

To: saramalone326@gmail.com

From: jadadragonNY@gmail.com

Dear Mom,

It's me, your daughter, Jada. I'm attaching a picture so
you know what I look like now. Dad gave me the earrings
I'm wearing in the photo. He's nice and generous,
and he's still just as handsome. Lots of ladies like him
(including this annoying new art teacher named Mel),
but I think he still loves you. We both do, I guess.

We just moved to Utah, and it's way better than you'd
expect. I'm writing to you because I was thinking you
could come out here. We have a whole house all to
ourselves! We're fixing it up super nice and colorful,
and Dad says all the movie stars come here every year.
So you'll probably be headed this way soon anyway.
Or I can come see you. Either one works.

Anyway, I hope even if you can't come yet, you'll write
me back.
Love,
Jada

Jada knew she wasn't much of a writer. She wished she could send her mom a picture of *Salt in My Wound* and tell her, *See this. Look at this. Now you know how I feel here without you.*

But since her dad's classroom was ready, Jada wouldn't be able to get the painting back from Mel until school started. This message couldn't wait that long.

Finally, Jada forced her hovering finger to hit Send. She trapped a big breath in her lungs and thought about all the things her mom might say back to her. *I missed you. I'm coming.* And maybe even the big one. *I love you too.*

Jada stared at the inbox. Every time she blinked, she kept her eyes closed a little tighter and a little longer, hoping that might give her mom enough time to hit her own Send button. She let herself imagine that her mom had been sitting at her computer at that very moment, wishing she knew how to find her daughter.

Patrick tapped the handle of his putty knife on Jada's door as he came into her room, right in the middle of the longest, tightest blink yet. "Everything okay? You got something in your eye?"

Jada closed out her email and shut the laptop. "I'm good. Can we paint the walls yet?" Painting would be the perfect job to keep her mind off her message, and it would help the house look nicer just in case her mom came soon.

"That's what I wanted to tell you. The living room and the kitchen are ready. If you start out there, I'll patch up and tape in here."

After prying the lid off one of the cans of buttery yellow, Jada poured a little into the pan. It looked like cake batter, and if it hadn't had the new paint smell, Jada might have been tempted to dip her finger in and take a taste.

Jada always did the rolling first—the fast, easy, fun part, where you could see a difference with every stroke. She'd wait until her dad started helping before she tackled the slow, boring work of corners and edges.

Once the roller had settled into the paint, Jada spun it across the tray. She didn't even bother with a drop cloth anymore. After painting five apartments already, she never dripped. She lifted the roller and placed it against the wall. This was it. The First Roll.

The First Roll was always the best part of painting—seeing that one patch on the wall, imagining how much better things would look after just a few hours. Painting a room was so much simpler than painting a canvas, and sometimes it was even more satisfying.

Jada rolled out all the paint she could, then stepped back to admire her work. She dipped in for the second roll (which was almost as good as the first, although she didn't capitalize it in her mind). Before she knew it, the whole wall was yellow and she'd lost count of how many times she'd reloaded.

Jada was so focused on her fresh yellow wall that she didn't notice her dad coming up behind her. So when he called her name, she jumped backward, tipping over the just-filled tray and spilling paint across the carpet and all over her legs.

"Patrick! What the heck?" Jada scowled, wanting to put the blame on her dad as soon as possible so he'd forget that she was the one who'd tipped the tray and chosen not to use a drop cloth.

"Sorry I scared you." Patrick reached for a rag. "But weren't we going to do green in the living room and yellow in the kitchen?"

Jada's stomach dropped. She'd been so excited to get started that she'd forgotten her whole color plan. But Patrick was right. He was right and she had ruined the carpet and her mom might never answer her. He was right and she was stuck in Utah and she didn't have any friends, except maybe the garden girl and the restaurant girl. But even those were a stretch.

Jada didn't know if she could stand to be wrong about the paint colors, so she made up a new truth. "I did it on purpose. I thought the yellow would be better in here. Can't we put the green in the kitchen?"

Patrick bent over the floor and scooped up all the paint he could with the rag. It didn't look anything like cake batter anymore, not with dirty chunks of carpet fuzz sticking out of it.

"We can put the green in the kitchen, but we don't have enough yellow to cover this whole room. And I don't think we can return the extra green. Could we do one green wall in here?"

Jada's sour stink face was all the answer Patrick needed.

"Well, I guess we can use the extra green in the bathroom. But we might have to wait until I get paid to buy more yellow."

Jada grabbed her own rag and frowned as she wiped the paint from her legs. Five apartments painted and she'd never made a mess like this. The whole place was cursed after all. Cursed and lonely. Only her mom could help her escape it.

When Jada's legs were paint-free, she grabbed a new rag and helped her dad scrub. The carpet was so old that strands came up every time she swiped at it. She was about to suggest they give up and cover the spot with a table or a rug when somebody knocked at the door.

"I'll get it." Jada jumped up and tossed her rag into the corner. She was more than ready for a distraction. But she wasn't ready to face the person she found on the front porch.

Mel.

Mel in clothes so ugly and splattered, they had to be her painting clothes.

Jada was about to tell Mel they were okay without her help, but Mel didn't give her the chance. She turned and sprinted back through the wind instead. "I almost forgot!" she called as she reached to grab something from inside her car.

Salt in My Wound. Jada wondered if she could send a picture of her salty tree painting to her mom now, or if she should wait until her mom wrote back first. *Things I never thought I'd think: If only Mel had come over a little sooner.*

Mel ran back up the steps two at a time, struggling to keep the painted side of the canvas angled barely away from the wind. She stepped inside and handed the painting to Jada, who couldn't help but notice that not one grain of salt fell from the surface.

"I wondered," Mel said, looking Jada straight in the eye, "if you'd be willing to display it at Back to School Night next week. We're inviting the whole community so they can see what we're about. There will be performances too, but we definitely want some artwork on display."

Jada slumped onto the couch with the canvas in her lap. "Isn't that cheating?" she asked. "Like the school's taking credit before they've even taught us anything? And how can it be Back to School Night if nobody's gone to school there yet?"

"Jada," Patrick warned.

But Mel just laughed. "Good point. I hadn't thought of it as cheating, but maybe it is, a little. Mostly we want everybody to see the school and get to know each other. Are you in? I don't want to make you do something that feels like cheating."

Jada pictured a small crowd gathered around her painting, admiring her work. "I guess you can show it. If you want to." She thought of her drawing from the library garden. "I might have another one soon that's even better."

"Great! We'll plan on it." Mel turned to Patrick. "Have you checked your email? They finally paid us."

Jada jumped from her seat. "Hey, does that mean we can buy more yellow now?"

Patrick nudged Jada with his elbow. "I guess we'll have to, huh? Mel, do you want to come with us to the paint store?"

Eww, no. We're not all going together like we're a family. Jada had to get herself out of this one ASAP. "I'll just stay here and keep working. Green in the kitchen, right?"

Mel peeked into the kitchen. "That will look great! I think most people would have put the yellow in the kitchen, but how boring would that be? Green is much more original." She smiled at Jada. "I'll stay here and paint too, if that's okay."

Jada had to stop herself from squeezing her canvas too tight. Boring? Her original plan for yellow in the kitchen would have been *boring*? To *Mel*?

"Sounds good to me. I'll leave you two alone, then." Patrick picked up his keys and gave Mel a shouldery side-hug. "Thanks again for helping out." Then he looked deep into her eyes. "I mean it. Thanks so much."

Jada had already rolled most of the living room walls

and hadn't gotten a single thank-you. Were Patrick and Mel dating? Then even creepier thoughts snaked into Jada's head. Had Patrick brought Jada to Utah to replace her mom? To replace Jada herself?

No way was she going to let that happen. Jada grabbed her flip-flops and followed Patrick out the door. "I changed my mind. I want to come to the paint store."

Patrick frowned. "You'll have to talk to Mel eventually. Might as well start now." He climbed into the car and looked back up at Jada from the driver's seat. "Give her another chance, okay? I'll be back in half an hour." He shut the door and started the engine.

Jada actually considered giving Mel one last chance, just so Patrick would give it a rest. But when she walked back through the door, Mel wasn't in the living room. She was in the kitchen, holding Jada's sketchbook and breaking Jada's number-one rule: *Nobody sees my work until it's finished.*

Apparently Mel didn't know the rules or care about other people's privacy. She looked up when Jada came through the doorway. "Is this the one you were telling me about? It's not bad at all. Almost reminds me of Cassatt."

Jada snatched the sketchbook from Mel. "I'm not

finished! Nobody can see my work until it's finished. It's bad luck."

Mel frowned. "What about your teachers? How did they teach you anything?"

Jada wasn't sure about that one, which made her want to get away from Mel even more. "That's it. I'm out." She slammed the cover of her sketchbook and jammed all her supplies into her bag, including the treasure box.

"Wait, Jada," Mel pleaded. "Where are you going?"

"To the library. I'll leave a note for Patrick, but he won't care. He lets me go there all the time."

Mel followed Jada to the door. "It's so windy. Let me drive you."

"I don't need a ride. I'll take the train." Jada didn't know where any bus stops were, but she and Patrick passed the train station every day, and the tracks led straight to the library.

"Please, Jada. Don't go." Mel reached for Jada's arm. "I'll go. You don't have to be the one to leave. This is your home."

Jada jerked her arm away from Mel. "Just stay. Paint it whatever color you want! I can tell you'd love to move in."

With that, Jada closed the door between her and Mel,

between her and the paint and the work and the mess. She walked away, past the houses and the apple trees and corners where the lemonade stands would be if this blasted wind storm would stop. She bowed her head and walked until the strap of her sandals cut into her ankles, until the football stadium appeared with the train station beside it. Jada had just enough time to buy a ticket before the next train left for downtown.

Even though she'd never taken the train by herself, Jada was too mad to be nervous about it. She only wished the tracks would somehow turn around and take her over the mountains and straight to her mom.

But the train just glided west, so Jada gave up and leaned her head against the glass. Her only hope was that her real ticket out of here—a message from her mom— might be waiting in her inbox. Maybe her mom had had a chance to answer while Jada was painting the living room and dealing with Mel.

When the train screeched into her station, Jada jumped from her seat and hurried into the library, straight downstairs to the children's level. She handed the book box back to the librarian in case that would make her wish official, then hustled back up to the computers on the main floor.

Unfortunately, the computers were full. Every single one of them had a person sitting in front of it, staring and clicking. She waited a few minutes to see if anybody would leave, but they all still stared, zombie-eyed, at their screens.

There have to be more computers in this place. Jada sort of remembered seeing some down on the children's level. She was so anxious to check it out that she didn't notice the girl with the tangerine hair until she almost crashed into her.

"Hey!" Jada shifted her bag on her shoulder, torn between wanting to talk to the girl and needing to check her email. "Thanks again for letting me draw you. I'll have to show you when the big version's finished—it turned out pretty good."

Jada hesitated, hoping the girl would speak this time. But the girl just nodded, and another layer of disappointment settled on Jada's shoulders.

"See you around," she said, leaving the girl on the stairs. She told herself it didn't matter anyway, that she and the girl couldn't have been friends because she'd be leaving soon to live with her mom. But part of her still wished they'd found a way to really talk to each other.

Jada sat down at the closest computer and let her knees bounce under the desk as the computer woke itself up. She found the page and logged in to her email as quickly as her fingers would move, then held her breath as she waited for the inbox to appear.

1 new message: saramalone326@gmail.com

With a trembling hand and a thumping heart, Jada clicked on her mom's message and began to read.

Chapter 15

THE WIND STILL howled as Malia spelled out the daily specials on the restaurant chalkboard. She frowned at the uneven letters and blobbish flowers she'd drawn. She'd have to do better than this (and not set off any more smoke alarms) if she wanted to prove to her family that she wasn't a strain.

Malia's dad glanced at the board and gave her shoulder a squeeze. "Looks good to me. Let's get out of here." Malia added her signature M-W butterfly in the bottom corner, then brushed the chalk dust from her hands. She was definitely ready to go home.

But when they passed the turnoff, her dad got a sneaky grin on his face. "Guess where we're going?" he asked.

"Um, the hospital?" It wasn't much of a guessing game.

Malia's dad nodded. "And guess what you get to do?"

"Take Mom home?" Malia crossed her fingers, but her dad shook his head.

"Not today, but this is just as good." He held his breath like he was waiting for her to guess again, but he couldn't keep it in for long. "You get to hold the baby! She's been stable forty-eight hours now, so you can come right in with me!"

"Oh, wow." That actually was a surprise. Malia bit her bottom lip. If she wanted to be a doctor someday, she'd have to do much scarier stuff than holding barely-there babies. So why were her hands starting to sweat?

When they reached the glass doors with all their

warnings, Malia hesitated. It still felt like passing through here might be breaking a rule. "I don't know if I'm ready. She's so tiny. What if I do something wrong?"

Malia's dad squeezed her arm. His hands were so big and strong compared to hers. "Don't worry about it. We'll show you what to do. Just be extra gentle with her, since her skin's super fragile and sensitive. Try not to bump the wires or tubes too much. Oh, and make sure you always support her head really, really well."

How was she supposed to remember all those things at once? Malia stood at the hospital sink and scrubbed her hands and arms and even under her fingernails. She rubbed her hands with sanitizer, just like her dad. But even scrubbing *and* sanitizing didn't seem like enough.

When Malia's mom looked up from the baby and beckoned her in, Malia thought she might belong behind the big doors after all. "There's my girl," her mom whispered, smiling straight at Malia. "I've been missing you all morning." She nodded at the chair next to her. "Sit down and put your arms in front of you, like you're hugging an invisible version of me."

Malia followed her mom's instructions, and before she

could even look up or ask what came next, her mom set the small bundle in her arms.

After that, Malia didn't want to look up. She felt the soft warmth of the blanket against her skin, but the baby didn't seem to weigh anything at all.

When Malia paid attention, she could feel a slight shift in the blankets as the baby breathed in and out, in and out, with the help of the oxygen tube in her nose. The baby's fingers curled delicately around the edge of the blanket, with perfect little nails that already looked like they might need a trim. Her skin was almost see-through, especially around her nose, and Malia could see the tiny veins underneath. She held her sister a little closer and inhaled, breathing in a scent so much better than anything she'd ever smelled at the hospital before.

The baby's eyelids fluttered open, just for a second, and Malia and her sister really saw each other for the first time. Malia had hoped she would be able to love her baby sister—and she did, instantly and deeply.

But the thing that surprised her was how fierce her love could be. *I'd do anything to keep my baby sister safe*, she realized. *Anything*.

"Did you forget the rest of us were here?" Malia was

startled by her dad's voice and his gentle laugh. "Do I get a turn sometime today?"

Malia sank deeper into the chair. She wasn't sure how long she'd been holding the baby, but she wasn't ready to give her up. "In a minute. I'm trying to think of a name for her."

Her mom sighed. "You can hold her as long as it takes if you'll come up with the right name. Nothing quite fits."

"We were going to give her the most beautiful name in the world," her dad said with a wink, "but then we realized we already gave it to you."

Malia smiled as she breathed in her baby sister's scent. "Don't worry," she said, barely touching the dark wisps of hair on top of the baby's head with the tips of her fingers. "Now that I know her, I'll figure something out."

Malia was still puzzling over the name as she practiced the harp that evening. Her parents were right—nothing quite seemed to fit. She was just wondering whether any music words might work—Melody? Aria?—when her dad burst through the door.

"I've got to go to the hospital," he said, the fear written across his face. "The baby's not breathing right. They think something irritated her lungs. Kiana will be here as soon as her class is over."

Malia tipped her harp up. "I'm coming. I can help." She wasn't a doctor yet, but neither was her dad. It was time to keep the promise she'd made to protect her baby.

But her dad shook his head. "They won't let you back to see her now anyway. I'll call as soon as I know anything new." He hesitated. "I'm sure everything will be fine."

He didn't look sure. But before Malia could even argue, he planted a kiss on her forehead and was gone.

How could Malia protect her sister if they wouldn't even let her come to the hospital? She tried to keep practicing her harp, but that wasn't helping anybody. She tried to clean the kitchen, but she wasn't sure where to start. Malia shut the dishwasher a little too hard.

She had to do *something*.

Malia scribbled a note for Kiana and left it on the kitchen counter. She grabbed a jacket to protect herself from the wind that still hadn't given up outside. Then, with the treasure box poem and its colorful envelope tucked in her pocket, Malia fought the fierce winds all the way to the cathedral.

Organ music, soft and sad, washed over Malia as she

pulled open one of the cathedral's heavy, carved doors. She chose a seat on one of the hard wooden benches and clasped her hands together. But as Malia bowed her head to say a prayer, she noticed something terrible.

"No," she whispered. "Oh, no."

Malia covered her chest with one hand, wishing she could change what she saw spread across her shirt—sprinklings and streaks of chalk dust.

It was all her fault. Malia hadn't changed her shirt after writing the specials on the chalkboard. She hadn't worn the smock the nurse had offered her. And now there was chalk dust in her baby sister's lungs and she couldn't breathe.

Suddenly, Malia couldn't breathe right either. She clutched the bench and searched her mind for somebody else to blame. Her mom had put the baby in Malia's arms before she was ready. Her dad had insisted that nothing would go wrong. And look what had happened.

Malia bowed her forehead to the bench in front of her, her guilt growing with every breath. There were scattered worshipers and hushed voices all around her, but Malia had never felt so alone. She closed her eyes and waited for the words of a prayer, but all she could think of was the tiny person she'd held in her arms and how much she wanted to watch that baby grow.

But as much as she'd wanted to help, Malia had only made things worse. Instead of protecting her baby sister, she'd hurt her. Malia was dangerous to her family, and a liar. She had to figure out a way to stop messing up and actually start helping, since her promises and prayers hadn't gotten her anywhere at all.

Malia remembered the poem in her pocket, the one she'd gotten when she found the box at the hospital before the baby was even born. She unfolded the homemade envelope, hoping this treasure could give her guidance somehow. Then, for the first time, she noticed the words on the front.

Evergreen Academy.

There it was, all glossy and colorful in her lap: a brochure for the very school Miss Rousseau wanted her to sign up for. The one that would mean leaving her home and her mom and her baby sister all day, every day, and letting them have a whole special life together that she couldn't be part of.

Malia tried to ignore the ache in her chest as she dropped the brochure and picked up the other piece of paper. She smoothed the poem against the bench and began to read.

Into My Own
by Robert Frost

One of my wishes is that those dark trees,
So old and firm they scarcely show the breeze,
Were not, as 'twere, the merest mask of gloom,
But stretched away unto the edge of doom.

I should not be withheld but that some day
Into their vastness I should steal away,
Fearless of ever finding open land,
Or highway where the slow wheel pours the sand.

I do not see why I should e'er turn back,
Or those should not set forth upon my track
To overtake me, who should miss me here
And long to know if still I held them dear.

They would not find me changed from him they knew—
Only more sure of all I thought was true.

Even though it made the ache grow stronger, Malia knew she'd found her answer. She had to go out into her own, and that meant going to the school. She'd been willing to lie to stay home another year, but it was time to face the truth.

A good daughter would print the papers and fill them out in her very best handwriting, then practice as long as her fingers would let her to show Miss Rousseau she was ready. So that was exactly what Malia would do. That way, her mom wouldn't have to worry about Malia anymore. She could spend all her worry and love on the baby instead.

As she strode down the aisle of the cathedral, Malia knew her path would go deeper into the world. She'd just have to hope and trust that, after a while, her family would follow behind. That they would forgive her for all the mistakes she'd made, and still hold a place for her in their hearts.

Now there were too many things to pray for. Before she left the cathedral, Malia lit a candle and whispered them all. Then she wrapped her arms around herself and prepared for the storm outside.

Grace

Chapter 16

GRACE SAT IN the backseat of Aunt Mona's car and clutched her bag to her chest. As they circled the parking garage, the ceiling seemed to get lower and the aisles narrower. Too many cars down here meant too many people up above, and even though Grace didn't know the details of Aunt Mona's plan, she knew it would involve talking.

If only she could make Aunt Mona understand that

she *wanted* to talk. It wasn't that Grace didn't think words were important. The problem was, they were so important she couldn't bear to get them wrong.

Aunt Mona dragged Grace through the thick heat of the parking garage and into the current of shoppers. "Let's see. I could use some foot scrub. Which way, Grace?"

Grace wasn't sure what foot scrub was or where to buy it. She raised her shoulders an inch to tell her aunt she didn't know.

"Well, find out please." Aunt Mona gestured to the information desk, where a teenage boy sat flicking paper clips into a cup.

Grace approached the desk. The boy looked up without really raising his head or stopping his paper clip game. "Welcome to City Creek. Can I help you?"

Grace nodded. *Maybe he'll just keep asking yes or no questions.*

"Okay. *What* can I help you with?"

Maybe not.

The boy began unbending one of the paper clips. Grace wondered if she could write him a message, but the only things on the desk were the paper clips and the cup.

She didn't dare bring out her poem book in front of Aunt Mona.

Grace tightened her fists and tried to swallow.

Six words.

Just say, "Where can I buy foot scrub?"

Say those six words and you'll be done.

But Grace couldn't fool herself. She knew it wouldn't be that easy. The boy might not know what foot scrub was either, and then she'd have to ask someone else. And once they found the foot scrub, if foot scrub even existed, Aunt Mona would just make more demands. It might never end.

Grace's breathing became fast and shallow as the fear snaked under her skin. She needed someone to save her from this, to make Aunt Mona go away. She needed her mother. But Grace had been so mad at her mother for abandoning her that she'd left her phone at home.

The noise of the crowd seemed to grow as the fear clouded Grace's vision. All she could see was the paper clip boy and the hopeless task in front of her. She felt a piercing pain in her side as Aunt Mona pinched her through the fabric of her shirt.

Aunt Mona leaned closer and whispered in Grace's ear.

"You're embarrassing yourself and embarrassing me. Ask him where the bath and body store is."

The boy put the paper clip down and reached under the desk. "Dude, do you just want a map or something?"

Grace nodded gratefully and reached forward to take the map, but Aunt Mona swiped it from the boy's hand. "She doesn't need a map. She needs to ask you a question."

The boy raised one eyebrow. "Are you her mom?"

Aunt Mona gave a short bark of a laugh. "Thankfully not."

"Then step back and wait your turn." The boy beckoned Grace closer and handed her another map. "If she were my mom," he whispered, "I'd run away."

Grace tried to smile at the boy, knowing it was the only way she could thank him. She stuffed the map into her bag as Aunt Mona's fingers closed around her arm again. "We'll try this again when we get to the bath and body store."

As Grace looked down the long rows of stores and the endless swarms of people moving between them, her heart began to pound so hard she could feel a pulse behind her eyes.

I can't do this.

The sweat along Grace's spine began to bead and drip.

She'll make me talk to every single one of them, and when I can't, she'll hurt me.

The crowd came into sharper focus, moving and laughing and seeming to multiply. Every voice was a sharp reminder that Grace couldn't speak. She could barely drag enough air into her lungs to breathe. And then, just when she thought the fear would swallow her whole, she thought of the boy's words.

I'd run away.

If she wasn't safe, she could run away. Not for good, of course. Just until her parents came home and she could tell them what was wrong.

But for now, she didn't need to say a word. She only needed to run.

Grace lunged, shoving her shoulder hard into Aunt Mona's chest. Mona shrieked, losing both her balance and her grip on Grace's arm.

The second she was free, Grace broke into a run. She dodged the crowds and signs and benches, ignoring the murmurs of surprise and Aunt Mona's shouts behind her. She pushed her lungs and legs until they begged her to stop.

But Grace didn't slow down until she was out of the mall and across the street and sure she hadn't been followed. She ducked behind a bench and folded herself up, hugging her arms around her knees and trying to make herself as small and unnoticeable as possible. Grace closed her eyes and rested her head against her arms for forty-eight breaths, each one a little longer and more relaxed than the one before it.

Once she looked up, Grace realized she had no idea where she was. It wasn't a comforting feeling, exactly, but if she didn't know where she was, Aunt Mona probably didn't either.

Grace took in the brick wall and the flower beds around her. A gray building rose in front of her—not the temple with its golden angel, but one with sharp, white spires all around that looked like they could protect her.

Part of her wanted to panic, but Grace counted her breaths and insisted to herself that she was in control now. She smoothed the mall map and studied it until she felt sure she wasn't on it anymore. All these flowers and trees and the white-spired building weren't part of the mall, and Grace knew she'd crossed a street. So even though she couldn't see the temple, this must be Temple Square.

A tour group passed in front of Grace's bench, and she tagged along behind, happy to listen and not feel so alone. As they rounded the corner of the white-spired building, Grace saw the golden angel against the sky and knew she was right.

Temple Square. Grace's parents used to bring her here every Christmas to see the millions of colorful lights, but that tradition had faded now that Decembers were filled with hospital fund-raisers for her mom and end-of-semester catch-up for her dad.

The grounds of Temple Square looked totally different in the heat of summer and the light of day, when the flashes of color were growing in the flowerbeds instead of glowing in the trees. It felt different too, when your parents were across the country instead of holding your hands. And how was it possible that the wind was barely blowing here?

Grace stayed with the tour group as long as she could, trying to blend in and keep an eye out for Aunt Mona. When the tour finished and there was still no sign of her aunt, Grace relaxed a little. She settled down in a shady spot near a fountain to survey her supplies.

Two granola bars, eight dollars, her library card, and

the small CD player. Underneath those, Grace's poetry book and pencil.

And one more thing—the treasures. Of course, the CD was there, but Grace had almost forgotten about the painting she'd pulled out of the box. At first, it reminded her of a picture she'd seen at church, where Mary Magdalene washed Jesus's feet.

But as Grace looked a little closer, she realized it was something else entirely. As she focused on the glow of the figures' faces and the softness of the brushstrokes, Grace felt the sharp edges of her worry melting away. The painting wasn't of a Bible scene after all, but of a mom washing the feet of her little girl. The girl was nice and round, just like Grace used to be, and her mom loved her. That was clear.

Grace laid the tips of her fingers against the mother and child. *We used to be like this.*

When had everything changed? Grace remembered a picture from her baby book, one where her mom smiled straight at the camera with a laughing, towel-wrapped Grace in her arms and soap bubbles dripping from her elbows. Even though her baby book was home in her living room, Grace didn't need to look at it to remember the words her mom had written under that photograph. "Love you forever." In spite of all that had happened, Grace still believed those words.

Things have *changed. But maybe they can still change back.*

A sudden screech of traffic outside the wall reminded Grace that right now she needed to take care of herself. Going home wasn't an option until her parents were there. But where could she go?

Temple Square felt welcoming and safe in the daytime, but they locked the gates at night, and Grace had heard the tour guide say that gardeners came in the very early morning to tend to the grounds. Before the sun set, she'd have to find a safe place to spend the night.

So after another hour of wandering quietly, reading plaques, and listening to bits of tour guide speeches in a dozen languages, Grace left the shade of Temple Square. She wasn't sure which bus routes she was near, but there was a train station just outside the gates. According to the TRAX map, three stops on the blue line and a quick switch to the red would take her right to the only place that seemed safer than Temple Square: the library.

The rumble of the train matched the rumble in Grace's stomach, and she knew two granola bars wouldn't be enough to last the night. She stepped from the train and stopped to think. The library had its own coffee shop, but Grace needed something more.

Just then, Grace's gaze caught the logo of her family's favorite Hawaiian restaurant from down the street. She had never known this was where the actual restaurant was. She'd only accepted the food when it was delivered to her doorstep. Maybe tasting the familiar flavors in the library would make it feel a little more like home.

It wasn't until Grace stepped up to the to-go counter that she realized her problem. How could she order if she couldn't speak?

A girl with black hair and very white teeth smiled down at her. "What can I get for you?"

Grace's mouth dried out and her knees buckled. She wanted to run away, but her stomach reminded her that she was already hungry and had a long night ahead. Her eyes darted around the room and landed on the chalkboard, where there seemed to be a picture message just for her.

The heart-winged butterfly. The very same one from the CD, and the sugar at the hospital. Grace looked around for the girl as she reached her fingers toward it.

"You want the special?" the waitress asked.

Grace nodded. The special was less than eight dollars. The special would be perfect.

Ten minutes later, Grace had braved the wind all the way to the library and hidden the food in her bag. She passed through the main doors right before closing time and snuck downstairs and into the bathroom. Just as she balanced her feet on the toilet seat in the very last stall, the bathroom door opened.

"Hello?"

Grace recognized the voice of the man who worked at the children's circulation desk. She held her breath and pressed the flap of her bag closed, hoping the air freshener smell of the bathroom would hide the scent of her food.

"I thought somebody came in here. The Andrews girl with the red hair."

He knows my name? Even though she was hiding, Grace had never felt she belonged in the library as much as she did in that moment.

"She left hours ago. Such a lovely child." Hazel was here too!

"Well, I think we're clear. Have a good night, Hazel."

"Good night, John. See you tomorrow."

Just when Grace had started to wonder if it was safe

to come out, she heard the creak of the door again and another voice, much younger than Hazel's. "Stay put. I've got your back." The voice was familiar, but it was hard to recognize when it was just a whisper. "Everything's going to be okay, you know. Remember this truth: you are not alone."

But with a click of the light switch, Grace was alone. Still, she trusted the voice and the words from the box. So Grace waited until there were no more footsteps above her, then waited even more. In the dim glow of the emergency light, she counted the rows and columns of tiles in her stall and turned them into multiplication problems. She mouthed the words to the Pledge of Allegiance and "The Arrow and the Song" twelve times each. And when she was absolutely sure she was the only one left, Grace slid silently out of the stall.

The children's level looked strange when nobody was around, but it was still early, and enough light filtered in from outside that it didn't seem scary. Grace crept to the farthest corner of the reading attic and settled in.

The library always seemed like a quiet place, especially on the top floors, but now Grace realized how much quieter it could be. Too quiet, even for her. The packaging on her dinner seemed unbearably loud as she pulled it from her bag and opened it up.

Grace ate, careful not to leave even a drip or a crumb behind. As she thought of all the times she'd shared these same flavors with her parents, she wished she were at her own round table at home, with her dad 120 degrees to the left and her mom 120 degrees to the right. Grace suddenly missed her parents very much. She wondered if they might be missing her too, and she realized how worried they'd be if Aunt Mona had told them Grace had run away.

If she wrote her mom an email, though, she wouldn't worry. How many times had Grace done just that—told her mom where she was going and when she'd be home? When her dinner box was empty and her belly full, Grace threw away every bit of trash and made her way to one of the library computers.

The screen glowed through the darkness of the library as Grace found her mom's picture on the hospital's website. She clicked the blue Contact Me button under the picture and began to type.

Dear Mom,

I had to get away from Aunt Mona. I'm safe at

the library. I'll be home tomorrow.

Love,

Grace

Now Grace was ready to explore, just a little. Curiosity pulled her toward the lost and found drawer, but *Amicitia* wasn't inside.

The braided-hair girl must have taken the box home.

Grace smiled, hoping the girl had found her poem. She began to shut the drawer, but something caught her eye in the blank space the box had left behind. Something that definitely had not been there the last time she'd looked in the drawer. Grace took out the slick piece of paper, creased into perfect thirds. It wasn't her copy—she'd folded hers into an envelope and sent it away in the treasure box. But something about the Evergreen Academy brochure felt different this time.

Grace opened the brochure to the inside flap and found one beautiful sentence in the bottom section. "A world-class creative writing program with master teachers from across the country." Her mother must have forgotten that not all the arts involved performing. Grace certainly wasn't going to remind her.

The back of the brochure showed a beautiful old building, and Grace tried to imagine herself walking through its wide front doors. Now that she had left her fear behind, at least for a while, she wanted more than anything to *keep* moving forward. A fresh start at a new school seemed like it could be a very good thing. When the teacher called roll on the first day, the other kids wouldn't answer, "Grace is here, but she doesn't talk much," before she'd even had a chance to prove them wrong. To prove to herself that they were wrong. Since the school was new, the students would all be new together.

A little card attached to the brochure said there was an open house next week—right before school started. That would give Grace a chance to wander the halls, and maybe even a chance to find a friend. Suddenly, everything about Evergreen Academy seemed full of possibility.

Grace read the brochure again and gazed at its glossy pictures as she chose the softest-looking library couch for her bed. Now that she was full and safe, her body seemed to remember that she hadn't slept the night before, and seven o'clock seemed like a fine time to fall asleep. She slipped the butterfly CD into her dad's CD player and fitted the headphones into her ears, then lay back down on the bag that now made a perfect pillow.

The music began, reaching inside Grace and helping her mind paint memories of when she was young. The way she'd sneak into her mom's bed early in the morning, and her mom would wrap her arms around Grace and scoot over to give her the warm spot. The way her dad would let her stay up late if she'd watch baseball with him and read to her from his old comic book collection whenever she was sick.

As much as she wanted a best friend, Grace knew she wanted her parents back even more. She thought of the short message she'd written her mom and knew there was so much more to say. But now she wanted to say it all in person. And she was sure that once she saw her parents, the words would finally come.

Grace propped the mother-and-daughter picture up where she could see it, then settled back onto the couch. She listened to the song again and again until she felt herself drifting off. As she slipped the headphones from her ears and closed her eyes, Grace slid into a deep, dreamless sleep.

It was hours later that the sirens and shouting began.

Jada

Chapter 17

JADA CLICKED HER email closed and turned away from the screen, but it was too late. The words of her mom's message had already stung her eyes and burned themselves into her brain.

Jada,

Thanks for the email and the picture. Love those

earrings. It sounds like your dad and Mel are taking

good care of you. Your dad's a good guy, and if you

let him, he'll try anything to make you happy. But

that's the thing—nobody can make you happy. You

have to find it on your own, and I'm still searching.

That's why I can't come out there and, for now, you

can't come here either. I'm really sorry.

Take care of yourself and your dad. I wish I could, I

just can't. But I already know you're stronger than me.

Sara

Jada wanted to reply right away and set her mom straight about a few things (starting with who Mel was), but then she remembered Patrick's words. *The harder you try to hold on, the faster she'll run away.* The last thing she wanted was to scare her mom away for good.

Jada sat at the same back-corner library computer for almost an hour, logging in and out of her email, writing responses and deleting them, reading her mom's message and searching for something she'd missed or misunderstood. She was barely aware of the person who sat down next to her until that person reached over and put a wrinkly hand on top of Jada's, right over the keyboard.

"Would you like to take a break and think it over first?"

Jada pulled her hands away and eyed the old librarian. "Were you spying on me?"

The librarian laughed and pushed her chair back. "Oh, nothing as exciting as that, I'm afraid. I've just been waiting for a chance to talk to you, and you've stood up and sat back down three times already. I hated to interrupt you until I was sure interruption was what you needed."

Jada clicked out of her email again. "Okay. So what did you want to talk to me about?"

The librarian considered Jada. "Do you know Grace Andrews? The quiet girl with the long red hair?"

"I think so," said Jada. If the girl was just quiet, maybe she wasn't freezing Jada out after all.

"Well, she borrowed the treasure box after you brought it back, but she returned it right away. I wondered if you might like another turn." The librarian smiled, almost like she knew a secret. "I think perhaps she wanted you to have another turn. Friendship, you know."

The librarian pointed to the word on the book's cover.

Amicitia. Friendship. So that's what it meant. "Yeah, maybe." Jada had been so focused on her wish that she hadn't even thought about the word on the cover or finished figuring out the last treasure she'd found inside.

It hadn't seemed like much then—just a flyer for a concert the week before with a line of music circled at the bottom—but maybe it was important. Jada could read music a little from singing in the church choir with Grandma J, but she was scared of anything with that many flats. She pulled the flyer from her sketchbook and passed it to the old librarian. "Do you know what this means?"

The librarian looked it over. "*New World Symphony.* Well, I know the song. Dvořák wasn't American, but the symphony is for America, and he composed it when he lived in America. Often a new land can inspire us to do our very best art." The librarian turned the flyer over and began to hum a melody Jada hadn't heard since home. Her *real* home.

"What is that?" she whispered. "You know that song too?"

The librarian stopped and smiled. "Oh, it's written right here. It's my favorite part of the *New World Symphony.*"

Jada shook her head. "That's my grandma's favorite song. She sings it with her choir."

"The words came later, from one of Dvořák's students," the librarian said. "But you're right—same melody. Remind me how the first line starts."

Jada swallowed. She hadn't sung since coming to Salt Lake. "Goin' home, goin' home . . ." Her voice began to tremble, and she fought the tears gathering in her eyes. But she didn't stop singing.

The librarian joined in, her voice right on key and clearer than Jada had ever heard it. "It's not far, just close by, through an open door . . ."

People were turning their heads, but Jada didn't care. For the first time, she really felt connected to this strange place with its salt lakes and sugar houses. An image painted itself in her mind: the sun rising over mountaintops, and Patrick on the front porch of their new house, waiting for her with his arms stretched wide.

"Morning star lights the way, restless dreams all done;

"Shadows gone, break of day, real life just begun . . ."

When the song finished, Jada's tears finally spilled. "Thank you," she whispered to the old librarian. "I have to go now."

Back upstairs, Jada sat on a bench in the atrium and leaned back against the glass wall. She still missed her mom, or the memory of her anyway, and singing that song had made her realize how much she missed Grandma J too. So why did she suddenly feel like she needed to be in *this* place? Why had she pictured their run-down rental when she'd sung that song about going home?

Jada blinked away the last of her tears, then let her gaze drift up. Hundreds of tiny shapes dangled from the ceiling above her, but what were they? Books, maybe? And was there a bigger pattern?

Jada rode the glass elevator up to the third floor, keeping her eyes on the tiny books the whole time. As she rose, she knew she'd been right. They did make a bigger pattern, and it seemed to be pointed straight at her. *Is that what I think it is?*

When the doors opened, Jada rushed along the walkway to get a better look. Flights of stairs jutted out over the atrium, and Jada ran down half a flight, just to get as close as she could.

A shiver prickled the back of Jada's neck. The design was a head, and it was the most awesome, creepy thing she'd ever seen. The blank eyes seemed to stare straight through her. How had she never noticed the head before, formed by a thousand floating books?

Because I never looked up, I guess.

Jada leaned over the railing just a little. She'd been right—most of the small, sculpted shapes were books. But a lot of them were butterflies too. Some of them almost looked real, the way they gently fluttered their wings.

An old man in red suspenders joined Jada at the railing. "I can't decide if it's beautiful or spooky, the way it just stares like that. Can you?"

Jada nodded. "It's both. Art can be both."

The old man smiled and stood back up. "Right you are. If you're an art lover, young lady, follow me. I think you'd like the show we've got in the gallery. You ever heard of Minerva Teichert?"

Jada shook her head, and the old man rambled on about the exhibit as she followed him up the stairs. Weird as they were, she had to admit people in Utah were friendly. The man paused in front of the gallery and looked Jada over. "Do you aim to be a great artist yourself someday?"

"Yes, sir." It seemed like the right way to answer an old guy in suspenders.

"You'll stand out here, and that can be a good thing. But

don't worry. You'll fit in too. You look at these paintings, and you remember those butterflies. *All* those butterflies, all together." He tapped his temple. "You read me?"

"Yes, sir."

Jada spent the next two hours in the gallery, examining the paintings and reading the plaques. She hadn't finished studying them when the old man appeared beside her. "I'm sorry, miss, but we close at six on Saturdays."

"That's okay," Jada said. "I'll come back another time."

As she took one last look across the gallery, Jada felt like she'd recognize a Cassatt or a Teichert anywhere. But would somebody say that about her someday? *That's a Jada, I'd know it anywhere.* She thought of the two pieces she'd done since she came to Utah—the tree and the girl. They were so different, and maybe her best work ever, but was either one of them really *her*?

Jada wanted one last look at the creepy butterfly head before she left. But as she walked back down the floating stairs and looked toward the atrium, something else caught her attention.

It was the girl with the tangerine hair, shoving a white takeout container into her messenger bag and looking around very suspiciously. Jada hurried back to the main level but kept her distance. She spied as the girl snuck down the stairs and into the basement bathroom.

They're closing, but she's staying. I think she's staying here all night.

Jada was impressed, and a little concerned. If a girl that shy and careful was breaking a big rule in such a big way, she must have a good reason. If Jada could ask her what was wrong and promise to keep her secret, would the girl finally talk to her? And was she going to be okay?

Jada snuck toward the bathroom door, but the old librarian and one of her buddies beat her to it. She held her breath as they checked inside.

After several longer-than-usual seconds, the man let the door swing shut. He grabbed a water bottle and a set of keys from the desk, ready to leave.

But the old woman turned back toward the bathroom. If she went in there, the girl would be found for sure. Jada raced to the bathroom first and cracked the door open. "Stay put. I've got your back." She searched for the right words, and the right words seemed to be the ones from the box. "Everything's going to be okay, you know. Remember this truth: you are not alone."

Jada clicked the light off and let the door swing shut.

She stepped out just in time to intercept the old librarian.

"All done in there now. Yup. Hey, I have a question." Jada frantically tried to think of a question, but the librarian thought of a few for her.

"Are you all right, dear? Did you want your symphony flyer? Did you change your mind about the box?"

Jada nodded. "Yeah, the box! Could I borrow the box again, please? Right now?"

"Yes, of course. Let me get it for you."

The librarian shuffled to the desk, and Jada tried to zap a thought straight to the girl in the bathroom. *Stay put just a little longer.*

Jada took the box and thanked the librarian in her most polite voice. "Would you like me to walk you upstairs?"

The old librarian linked her arm through Jada's. "Oh, thank you, dear. I'd like that very much." She paused outside the girls' bathroom. "Do you smell pineapple?"

Jada forced a smile. "It's probably just my lip gloss," she said, wishing for the first time ever that her lips looked glossier. "Should we take the elevator?"

"My knees would appreciate that," said the old librarian.

They rode up together, then parted on the main floor. Jada had been so fascinated by the artwork and worried about the girl that she'd forgotten about her own troubles—until she saw Patrick waiting for her just inside the main doors.

Patrick ran to Jada and hugged her, then stepped back and let his hands weigh heavily on her shoulders. "Where have you been? You scared me, Jada."

"I've been in the gallery. Fourth floor. Patrick, have you ever heard of Minerva Teichert? Have you seen the creepy butterfly head?"

Patrick stepped back and folded his arms. "Jada, this is serious. I was worried about you."

Why didn't he think she was serious? When would he ever understand that art was serious to her? He really should have known to look in the gallery first.

Jada gripped the book box. "I didn't break any rules, Patrick. I've been here the whole time. I left you a note, and I told Mel where I was going."

"That was hours ago. I've been looking all over the place. I almost called the police. You can't just go running off when somebody makes you mad."

Now Jada was getting fired up all over again. "Why, because you think I'm just like Mom? Is that what Mel says?"

Patrick was speechless for a second, but Jada felt a lecture coming. The crowds were thinning and the guards were coming to lock the doors. "Forget it," she said. "Let's just go."

Patrick and Jada simmered silently as they drove home, until Jada noticed the car at the curb in front of their house.

"She's still here? Can't she take a hint?"

Patrick turned off the engine and clicked the locks shut. Jada knew she could just flick hers back open, but she was also smart enough to know that wouldn't be a good idea.

"She's a nice person, Jada, which is more than I can say for you right now."

Jada was too stunned to speak. *I am a nice person. I helped the girl at the library. I helped you with your classroom and I let myself get dragged around the country.*

Maybe the problem is I'm too nice.

Patrick wasn't finished. "I don't know what's going on with you, Jada. I feel like you've been in a bad mood ever since we came here. If there's something you want to talk about, let's talk about it."

Now Jada flicked the lock open. "I don't want to talk about it. Not with you and definitely not with her. I'll be in my room."

Patrick sighed. "You're not even going to help us paint?"

Jada climbed from the car and stood with one hand on the door. "You'll be fine. Now that you have Mel, you don't really need me anyway." She slammed the door and stormed inside, trying to block out Mel's happy humming as she painted the kitchen green.

As soon as Jada set the book box on her dresser, somebody knocked. Jada yanked the door open, ready to tell her dad to leave her alone. But it was Mel standing before her with streaks of green on her arms and even across her cheek.

"Can I come in?"

Jada didn't budge. "Why?"

Mel bit her lip and looked up. Was she trying not to cry? "I know about the email from your mom. And I'm so sorry."

Jada stared at Mel. "How do you know? Were you snooping in my account?" She reached for the doorknob to shut Mel out for good.

Mel shook her head and put her own palm on the door, ready to push right back. "I wasn't snooping. I . . ." Mel sighed and squared her shoulders. "We might as well get this all out in the open. Jada, I know because she told me."

Malia

Chapter 18

MALIA CLUTCHED THE Evergreen Academy brochure as she hurried home from the cathedral. The wind had finally slowed and softened, but she could tell from down the street that her house wouldn't be quiet or still. All four of her aunties' cars were squished into her driveway.

As Malia turned up the walkway, the curtains in the front window shifted. Five seconds later, little cousins began pouring out the front door with Kiana close behind. She pulled Malia into a hug and whispered, "The baby's much better. She's going to be fine. Your dad will give you the details when he gets home tonight." She gave Malia one last squeeze and slipped back into the house, leaving Malia alone with all the little ones.

"Were you really at the big church?" asked Kai.

"Yes." Malia scooped up Namea and sat on the front porch. She'd always thought of Namea as small and delicate. But after holding her baby sister, Namea seemed capable and sturdy and incredibly big.

"Why did you go by yourself?" asked Lexi.

Malia sighed. "Because I needed to figure some things out. It's quiet there."

"Will you take us?" asked Kala as she adjusted the wreath of ribbons in her hair.

"If you can ever learn to be quiet." She tickled Kala's knobby knees. "Why were you guys watching out the window?"

"We were waiting for you! And we're only allowed in the den. They're cleaning the rest of the house to surprise you."

A slap of guilt struck Malia. Hadn't she been keeping

the house clean enough? Was she an even worse daughter than she'd realized? Malia stood and helped Namea to the top step, still holding her hand. "I'm going to see if they need any help. You guys better get back to the den."

When Malia peeked into the kitchen, she realized how bad the mess had become. Dust covered the furniture and gathered in patches along the edges of the kitchen and hallways. Dirty dishes filled the sink and dotted the counter. The mail pile had grown too tall and tipped over, spilling across the family desk. The trash can overflowed and another full bag leaned against it. Malia had figured it would be easier to take the bags out two at a time, but now she saw and smelled why that wasn't such a good idea. She blushed as she overheard patches of conversation between her aunties.

"Eww, nasty! How long do you think this yogurt has been in here?"

"He'd never allow a mess like this in the restaurant. Thank goodness."

Just as Malia was about to step in and defend herself, she heard her own name.

"What would they have done without Malia?"

"Seriously. Sometimes I wonder what any of us would do without her. Did you hear the way the kids all rushed out there when they saw her coming?"

Kiana spoke next. "Think how lucky that baby will be to have her as a big sister." All the aunties murmured their agreement. "We should have come sooner, but it's thanks to Malia the whole place didn't fall apart this summer."

Now Malia's face flushed with pride. She hurried back to the den and was swallowed by a tide of tiny cousins. For the next hour, she hopscotched and wrestled and told funny stories, loving every minute of it.

But then the aunties knocked on the den door and began to sort all the little shoes onto the right little feet, even though Malia wasn't quite ready to see the cousins go. After lots of "one-last" hugs and kisses, Malia and Kiana were alone in the clean, quiet house. Kiana held up a thick chemistry book. "Do you mind if I study? Your dad will be here in an hour or so."

"Sure," said Malia. "I'll be upstairs if you need me."

Malia sat at her desk and read the music school brochure again with a heavy heart. In the calm of the cathedral, she'd been sure she could do it, sure that her family would be better off without her around all day. But everything had changed since she'd come home.

Did her aunties and cousins really need her? Did her parents? Was the baby really lucky to have Malia as a big sister? Leaving them every day seemed like exactly the wrong thing to do now. She'd love nothing more than to keep an eye on the baby while her mom made lunch, or to do homework with her sweet little sister in her arms. But Malia had made a promise to herself and her baby sister, and she had sort of promised it to God too. In a cathedral.

So Malia found the application online and spent the next hour working and writing. Once she'd filled in the whole thing, she closed her eyes and clicked Send before she could lose her courage.

Malia sat down at her harp, focusing on the music to help her prepare for the school, trying to make her fingers do just what they were supposed to do. When they finally did, Malia felt the same rising in her chest she'd felt in the cathedral that day. The Bach would have sounded almost like the CD if there had been a voice to go with it.

Malia kept practicing, even when she heard her dad's voice downstairs. She told herself to practice until he came for her, until she was needed or missed. And if it took a long time, then that would be a sign she'd done the right thing by applying for the school.

Just then, there was a knock at her door. Malia dropped her fingers from the strings, ready to remind her dad not to interrupt. "Come in."

But it was Malia's mom who came through the door. Malia stared for a second, then stood her harp up and raced across the room. Malia held her mom tight, surprised by how different it felt to hold each other now that there wasn't a baby bump between them.

After the longest, strongest hug of Malia's life, she finally let her mom go. There were so many questions she needed answered. "What are you doing here? Are you staying home now? Where's the baby?"

Malia's mom kissed her forehead. "I'm just here for a couple of hours, and the baby still won't be home for weeks. But she's going to be fine. She's strong, like you." She took Malia by the hand and led her downstairs. "Come see what we have for you."

In the kitchen, Malia's dad had lit candles and spread

the table with all the best dishes from the restaurant. "We wanted to have a special night, all three of us together. We wanted to thank you, Malia, for all you've done."

In the flickering light of the candles, Malia saw her home for exactly what it was: perfect. She didn't want to lose her place here, not ever.

But a thank-you dinner felt like another sign things were changing, and this time the sign was coming straight from her parents. Malia clutched her hands over her stomach. She thought of the mess in the kitchen earlier. Of the chalk dust and the baby's fragile lungs. Of the month she hadn't practiced her harp, and all the days before that when she'd whined about doing it.

She'd been selfish to delete Miss Rousseau's message and wrong to lie to her dad, but applying for a school they didn't even know about suddenly seemed worst of all.

Tears streamed down Malia's cheeks. She tried to remember the way she'd felt when her aunties talked about her, but those words just didn't seem true anymore. "I can't stop messing up."

Malia's parents looked at each other, then came to her. Each of them took one of her hands. Malia's mom looked straight into her eyes. "Honey, we're saying thank you."

Malia took her hand back and wiped her eyes, but her quiet tears quickly turned to sobs. Between gulping, gasping breaths, Malia choked out the words she'd been holding in all week.

"I'm sorry about everything. I'll be better. I know I should want to go, and some days I almost do, but I'm scared." Malia swiped her arm across her wet cheeks. "I'm scared to be there all the time, and I'm scared to not be here. Please don't make me go."

Her parents looked at each other like the other one should have the answer. Finally, they asked exactly the same question at almost exactly the same time.

"Go where?"

"There's a music school Miss Rousseau wants me to go to. I deleted the message and I didn't tell you, and I know that was wrong. I know I'm so, so lucky to even get a chance to go there. But I'll miss you too much. I'll miss the baby too much." The words poured out of Malia, even faster than her tears. "And what if I'm still a strain somehow? Miss Rousseau's parents sent her to music school in Paris!"

Malia's dad pulled her into his lap. "I never should have said you were a strain. Honey, Miss Rousseau is *from* Paris. And I talked to her about the music school today—it's only a few blocks away. We've passed the construction before. You can walk to school and bring friends over after to do homework. You can probably come home for lunch sometimes, and it's only as long as a regular school day."

"Wait, what?" Malia twisted to face him. "Really?"

Her dad nodded. "Remember the old Deseret Theater? They've added on and turned it into a school."

Malia's sobs faded to a few final tears as this new, wonderful truth sank in. The music school was right in her neighborhood? It was hard to believe the beautiful building she'd seen on the brochure was the same run-down theater where she'd played in her very first harp recital.

"That's it? Are you sure?"

Malia's dad laughed. "I'm sure. We'll drive by there tonight if you want."

"I love teaching you, Malia," her mom said. "And that will always be my job. I just want you to see how much more is out there."

"Okay," Malia said, and it almost seemed okay. Instead of being distant and scary, the new school had suddenly become close and familiar. Maybe finding the brochure in the treasure box even meant that she'd already know somebody there.

The three of them looked at each other and smiled. They wrapped each other in a Malia-sandwich hug. Then they realized the food was getting cold, so they loaded their plates and sat down to their feast.

Malia wanted this dinner to last forever. But soon the food was eaten, and the table was cleared. As her dad hummed and rinsed at the kitchen sink, Malia knew she needed to ask one more question that had been growing inside her. She needed to ask it before her mom left for the hospital again.

"Do moms love their first kid the same after the second one is born?"

When her mom didn't answer right away, Malia began to worry. She waited as her mom blew out all the candles but one, then lifted the one lit candle from the centerpiece.

"When I was a girl, I loved my family so much. Then I met your dad"—she bent forward and lit the candle on the left—"and I thought my heart was full. Just a few years later, Malia, you were born, and my heart must have grown, because I loved you every bit as much." Her mom lit another candle as Malia sniffled, already guessing what the last candle meant.

"Now this baby has come along. It doesn't change how

much I love you—not one bit. Can you see that?"

In the center of the table, Malia's flame still burned bright and strong. She nodded as her mom gave her a teary smile in the flickering light of the four candles. "I love our baby just as much as I love you. Not just the same, but just as much. Does that make sense?"

"It makes sense," Malia said. She loved her dad just as much her mom, but it didn't mean she loved them the same. And the fierce love she'd felt when she'd held the baby hadn't made her love her parents any less.

Malia's mom scooted her chair closer. She guided Malia's shoulders until Malia's head rested in her lap. Malia heard the catch in her mom's voice as she stroked her hair. "You will always be the one who made me a mom, and I can never thank you enough for that." She lifted her hand to wipe the tears from her cheeks. "Can I tell you one more thing?"

Malia nodded, blinking back tears of her own.

"If you ever go to Paris, you'd better take me with you."

Malia played the harp again that night, soaking up her mom's praise and listening to her suggestions.

"You really do play the Bach beautifully. I hope there's

someone at your new school who can sing it with you." She tucked Malia's hair behind her ear. "I hope your harp brings you happiness all your life."

"I want to be a doctor when I grow up." When the words were out, Malia watched her mom for signs of shock or disappointment or doubt. But all she saw was a proud, tearful smile.

"Then you will be, honey."

"A doctor who plays the harp?" Malia asked.

"Sounds perfect to me." Malia's mom eased down onto the bed and let out a long breath. "Now, what other big news have I missed?" Malia took the picture and the poem from her nightstand and told her mom the rest of the story of the treasure box. As she told it, Malia's dad came in and sat on the floor with his back against her bed.

"Will you ever find out who got the CD or your symphony flyer? Or who gave you these things?"

Malia shook her head. "I don't know. The library doesn't really keep track of it, but the old librarian might know." Now that her baby was safe and Malia wasn't scared of the new school, it suddenly seemed important to know where the picture and poem had come from and where the

CD and symphony flyer had gone.

"Do you think I might find them if I checked the box out again? Or at least find a clue?"

Malia's mom smiled. "I don't know. But your baby sister has taught me that even when something seems impossible, you always have to hope."

It was that very moment when Malia realized what her baby sister's name should be. As soon as she spoke it, her parents agreed. And for the rest of the night, no matter what Malia thought of—her baby sister, her new school, or even the girls from the library—Malia's heart was filled with Hope.

Grace

Chapter 19

GRACE JOLTED UPRIGHT when the alarm screamed.

Where am I?

What's going on?

Her confusion cleared a little as she looked around at the picture book shelves, familiar even in the dark. The alarm fell silent only a few seconds later, but it was followed by heavy footsteps, sharp-voiced shouts, and door bolts sliding open. Suddenly the whole building flooded with light, and one deep voice boomed above the rest.

"Salt Lake City Police!"

Grace grabbed her things. If the police were here, there might be a dangerous criminal in the building. Or what if they were here for her, and Aunt Mona was with them? What if they turned Grace over to her? She couldn't risk it. Grace slung her bag across her chest and sprinted for her bathroom stall.

The voices grew louder as the police came down the stairs, then spread across the children's level. Grace held her breath as the door to the restroom creaked open.

"Honey, are you in here?"

Grace knew that voice. She swallowed hard and closed her eyes. Then, for the first time in what seemed like forever, she spoke.

"Mom?"

Her mom wasn't supposed to be home for two more days, but when Grace scrambled out of the stall, there she was. They watched each other for only a moment, then met in the middle of the room and in each other's arms.

The bathroom door swung open and an officer peered inside. "Hey! There you are!" She propped the door open with her foot and called over her radio. "We found her, guys. Basement restrooms, near the main entrance." She snapped the radio back onto her belt and spoke to Grace.

"You okay?"

"I'm okay," said Grace.

The officer turned to Grace's mom. "This place is huge. How did you know where to find her?"

"I just had a feeling, and I followed it." Her voice broke. "For once, I followed it."

When they were home and snuggled under a blanket on the couch, Grace told her mom about Aunt Mona and her day alone in the city.

Grace's mom pulled her closer. "I can't tell you how sorry I am. But what you did was so dangerous. You've got to promise me you won't ever do anything like that again."

Grace nodded. "I promise." Now that she was safe at home again, now that she could speak again, she wouldn't need to.

"Good girl." Her mom kissed the top of her head. "Were you scared?"

Grace thought for a second. "Once I got away from Aunt Mona, I was barely scared at all."

"Oh, my brave girl." Grace's mom reached for her hand. "I feel like I hardly know you anymore. And that's my own fault."

Grace looked at her mom. Her usually-perfect hair was wrecked and her makeup had all worn away. But when they'd passed the big mirror in the front hall on their way to the couch, her mom hadn't even glanced in it. She'd been too busy asking Grace if she was cold or hot or hungry or sleepy.

"It's okay, Mom. You can get to know me again. I'll help you."

Grace's mom rested her head against the couch cushion. A sad smile wrinkled the corner of her eyes. "I want you to tell me everything, but especially the good parts. Did you say something about a treasure box?"

Grace and her mom stayed up the rest of the night, and Grace did most of the talking. They listened to "Ave Maria" again and again, and they both agreed it was their new favorite song.

Sunlight had started sneaking through the windows by the time Grace's dad came home. "I'm here, Grace," he whispered. "But you can rest. I'll still be here when you wake up, and whenever you need me after that."

He straightened the blankets over them, and Grace snuggled deep inside. "I missed you, Dad." She looked at the flecks of gray in her dad's hair. How long had they been there? And why hadn't she noticed? She had barely begun to wonder when her eyelids slipped shut.

The next thing Grace knew, she was waking up to the smell of hot chocolate and buttered toast and the sound of Giants baseball on the kitchen radio. Her mom was still beside her.

Grace told her stories all over again while they ate, and her parents promised that Aunt Mona was gone for good. By the time she'd finished the toast and the stories, Grace had lost count of the bites she'd taken, but she knew she'd never felt so perfectly full.

Grace smiled at the girl in the mirror. She looked so different in the pale blue dress her mom had chosen to set off her hair, now fixed in gentle waves around her shoulders.

I look almost grown-up.

Only a few days had passed since Grace's night in the library, but she could already tell her parents were going to keep their promise. Even tonight, they'd passed up a dinner party to be there for her Back to School Night. She'd never seen them so proud as when she'd volunteered to share a poem for the program.

Grace's mom peeked through the doorway. "We'll be in the car, honey, but take your time."

"Thanks, Mom. I'll be out soon."

The butterfly on Grace's necklace matched the ones in her stomach. She pulled her hair over her shoulder and took a deep breath. Even though she was still afraid, there were words in her blue book she just had to speak.

Grace's parents smiled at her as she slid into the backseat. Her dad backed out of the driveway, glancing at her in the rearview mirror. "Are you sure about this?"

Grace nodded. "I'm scared. But I'm sure too."

"You know we're proud of you no matter what," said her mom.

Grace knew. She was proud of herself too. The fear wasn't gone, but now she could stand up to it. She'd grown stronger than it. And tonight at her new school, she'd do something she never could have done before.

Tonight she was a whole new Grace.

Chapter 20

JADA STARED AT Mel. "What do you mean, she told you? My mom told you she emailed me?"

"Yes."

Jada wanted to tear things. Break things. But she wanted answers more. "You know my mom?"

"Yes."

"And you never told me?"

Mel stepped into Jada's bedroom and leaned against her dresser. "I tried, Jada, but it came out wrong. And you haven't really given me another chance."

Patrick appeared in the doorway. "Can I come in?"

"No!" Jada shouted. Her dad must have known about this all along. Why didn't anybody tell her anything?

Jada still liked Mel about as much as a kick in the shins, but at least she was finally spilling her secrets. "Leave us alone, Patrick."

Mel sighed. "We're good. Just give us a minute."

As Patrick retreated down the hall, Jada turned back to Mel. "Keep talking. And tell the whole truth this time. How do you know my mom?"

Mel pushed her lips together, like she was deciding where to begin. "Your mom and I were best friends in college. On the outside, we didn't have that much in common, but we just clicked. Sometimes the very best friends are like that. Your mom was all the things I wasn't—fearless and spontaneous and outgoing.

"Back then she liked having an anchor, and I gave her that, I guess. Then she met your dad, and he did the same thing. When you were born, I wasn't sure if I should help

236

out more or back off. Between the three of us, we might have made her feel too tied down."

Jada's head felt fuzzy. "You knew me when I was a baby?"

Mel nodded. "I did. You were hilarious. One day, when you were almost eighteen months old, your mom told me you'd never learn to walk. She said you'd probably side-step with your hands against the wall for the rest of your life. Well, you heard her. Right then, you pulled your hands off the wall and walked clear across the room. To me. I thought we'd never stop laughing."

Jada sat down on her bed, trying to sort it all out. She had seen a picture of herself in a bright blue sundress, smiling up at the camera with both hands against the wall. But she'd never heard that story. "So you're still friends with her?"

"As much as anybody is, I guess. I've been telling her all summer how talented you are. How brave and independent and bright you are. I've been trying to get her to reach out to you, and then at some point I realized you were old enough to do the reaching out. So I tried to help you."

Mel gave me the email address. Jada stared at Mel. Now

that she wasn't the enemy or even the nosy outsider, what was she? Without a word, Jada pulled up her mom's email on the laptop and passed it over to Mel.

Mel read the email and pressed a hand to her forehead. "Maybe I should have stayed out of it. I'm sorry, Jada."

"It's okay. At least now we know how to find each other if we want to."

Mel folded the laptop shut and handed it back to Jada. "She might spend her whole life looking for happiness. I hope she finds it."

"Me too." Jada thought about Mel's words, and suddenly she was afraid somebody would be saying the same thing about her someday. What if she had everything she really needed to be happy right here, and she spent her whole life looking instead?

Jada picked at her bedspread. She didn't want to keep anybody else from being happy either. "Are you going to start dating Patrick? I guess it's okay if you want to."

Mel laughed. "Thanks, Jada. But he's not really my type. We're just friends. I promise."

As they sat there in silence, Jada thought about all the ways Mel had helped her already, even when she didn't deserve it. Getting help from Mel didn't seem so bad anymore. "Hang on a second," she said.

Jada ran to the kitchen and grabbed her sketchbook. She held out the picture of the girl under the tree. "Will you look again? Will you tell me how to make it better?"

Mel took the picture from Jada and studied it. "This really does remind me of a Cassatt. It's lovely, Jada. But you're right—I think you can make it better." She held the picture straight out. "It would be a lot of work, but most of my favorite Cassatts are of more than one person."

Jada sighed. "I know. Moms and kids. I don't know if I want to stick the girl's mom in there."

Mel shook her head. "I don't want you to make it a Cassatt, though. I want you to make it your own. You'll figure out what's missing when you can picture what you want it to become." She checked her watch. "I think I'll leave you and your dad alone for a while. But definitely show this to me again, okay?"

Jada nodded. Even though she was tempted to figure out how to fix it right then, she knew her drawing would have to wait. It was time to help Patrick paint.

When Jada joined her dad in the living room, it looked

like a tornado had hit inside the house. The ugly carpet was ugly as ever, but now it was torn up in chunks all over the floor. Jada's jaw dropped. "What happened?"

Patrick yanked up another section of carpet and smiled at what he saw. "Good news, Jada. A little sanding and finishing and we're going to have hardwood floors."

"My room too?" Jada loved the idea of wiping up paint drips and sweeping pastel dust off smooth, shiny hardwood instead of putting an ugly drop cloth over the hideous carpet.

"We'll have to check, but probably your room too. They're in good condition everywhere I've seen so far." Patrick ran his hand along the grain. "Why anybody would staple polyester shag over solid oak is beyond me."

"Can I help?" Jada asked.

Patrick gestured to another polyester patch. "Be my guest."

Jada grabbed a corner of the carpet and ripped, again and again. She tossed the torn-up pieces into a dirty, fuzzy heap in the middle of the room. Jada didn't realize she was singing until Patrick stopped ripping and joined in with his deep baritone.

"Shadows gone, break of day, real life just begun . . ."

"Patrick," said Jada. She had to get the words out before she got all emotional again. "I'm glad you brought me here. I think this could be our home after all."

Patrick just smiled and kept singing. For the rest of the night, the two of them worked together, pulling away strips of shaggy brown to reveal something beautiful and lasting underneath.

Over the next four days, Jada painted (even the corners and edges) while her dad and Mel sanded and stained. The day they sealed the floor, Patrick kicked Jada out of the house so she wouldn't breathe in all the chemicals.

Jada carted all her art supplies to the backyard. It was time to add another girl to her drawing. Hours later, as she put the finishing touches on the trees around the second girl, Jada heard a voice calling over the fence.

"Hey, neighbor! Want an apple?"

It was the leader of the too-friendly moving crew. How had she never realized he lived right next door? The man plucked an apple from his tree and tossed it to Jada.

"Thanks." Jada thought of the box of apples he'd given them the first night and how she hadn't eaten a single one, afraid they might be poisoned. She wasn't really an apple person, but he was watching her with a goofy grin on his face.

Jada wiped the apple on her shorts and took a bite. It was crunchier than she'd expected, and just the right amount of sour.

Maybe I could be an apple person after all. Jada gave the man a thumbs-up as she chewed, and he shot one back at her and started up his lawnmower. She had just finished her snack when Patrick came out the back door, showered and shaved and wearing his best clothes.

"Are you ready to go? I told Mel we'd help set up for the program tonight."

Jada looked down at her messy art shirt. "Let me change first." She showed him the drawing. "What do you think?"

Patrick looked down and broke into a grin. "I love it! That looks just like you!"

Jada agreed. She'd never drawn herself in pastel before, but she had to admit that even a stranger would probably recognize her from this picture.

"Are you going to put one more person in at the top?" Patrick asked.

Jada socked him on the shoulder. "That's exactly what

I was thinking!" The composition was better now, but it still looked unfinished. One more girl would give it balance. One more girl, over near the first, and it would be complete. One more girl . . . like the girl from the restaurant, maybe.

Back inside, Jada scrubbed her hands and switched her dirty T-shirt and shorts for a bright blue dress. She hurried to the basement and sorted through the piles of stuff she'd stashed down there during all the home improvement adventures. Her fancy white sandals had to be somewhere.

Jada lifted a stack of Patrick's shirts and saw a book buried underneath. Not a book—the treasure box, which she'd completely forgotten about. *Oops.* A wave of guilt washed over Jada for keeping the box so long without even opening it.

When she finally found her sandals, she set them on the treasure box and brought it all upstairs. She'd drop the box off at the library tonight in case somebody else needed it. She couldn't think of anything to wish for now anyway.

Jada tore her pastel picture from the sketchbook and slipped it into a small manila envelope. She'd show it to Mel tonight and they'd figure out where the third girl should go. Jada slid the envelope through the crack between the book box and its cover to keep it from getting bent, then hurried outside.

"Patrick, can we stop by the library? Just for a second?"

He turned to face her as he started the car. "I told Mel we'd be at the school. We're kind of late already."

Jada held up the box. "This is overdue. I'll just run in and right back out. Please?"

Patrick sighed. "There won't be a parking spot."

"Drive around the block once, and if I'm not out waiting for you, leave me and I'll walk. But trust me, I'll be waiting!"

He shook his head. "Okay, okay. Once around the block. But you'd better make it."

Jada unbuckled her seatbelt a few seconds early. She braced the box against her chest with one hand and held the other over the door handle. As soon as Patrick pulled over in front of the library, she was off.

Jada sprinted to the front doors, then did an almost-rule-breaking racewalk down the stairs. After a quick glance around the room, she found the old librarian scanning books into the computer.

"Here's the box! I don't need it anymore. But thanks!"

She flashed a quick smile and left before the librarian could slow her down.

Jada moved even faster when she didn't have to worry about running with a maybe-fragile book box. She waited with a smug smile until Patrick had finished circling the block.

"Told you I'd make it," she gloated as she tried to catch her breath.

It wasn't until later, when she saw Mel set *Salt in My Wound* proudly on a display easel, that Jada realized she'd left her other picture in the box.

Malia

Chapter 21

MALIA HAD BEEN practicing "Ave Maria" all day for her big performance. She wanted to play it perfectly—for herself, for Miss Rousseau, and most of all, for her mom.

But no matter how many times she played it, there was something missing. The song didn't sound complete without the voice anymore, and Malia had started to forget the other part. Even when she had the music in front of her and told herself to follow it, there was a section in the middle that just wasn't right.

"It sounds beautiful up here!" Malia's mom came in and sat gently on her bed.

Malia wrinkled her nose. "If you say so."

"I do. But if you practice too much the day of a performance, you just psych yourself out. I think what you need is a distraction. Let's get you out of the house." Her face brightened. "Let's go to the library and see if the box is back! I need to return some books anyway. I'll pack up your harp while you get dressed."

Malia felt like a real musician when she put on the long, flowing blue dress and fastened the delicate harp pendant around her neck. She didn't even mind that her outfit might be a little out of place in the library.

The old librarian came toward Malia as soon as she passed through the main doors. "You look so lovely! I have a feeling you're here for *Amicitia*. It just came back in—let me get it for you."

Malia spotted the row of computers with headphones attached and had a new idea. "Thanks," she said. "I'll be right over there." Maybe if she listened to the song one more time, she'd remember the part in the middle.

Only she couldn't find the right arrangement. Malia's eyes stung with tears by the time her mom found her.

"This isn't going to work."

Malia's mom squeezed her hand. "You're supposed to *not* be psyching yourself out, honey. You'll be fine. You know the notes."

"I don't know them all! There's that line in the middle that's different. Once you know both parts, it doesn't sound right with just one."

Malia's mom leaned forward and looked straight into her eyes. "Bach is always good, even by himself. Some of his most beautiful work is for a single instrument. Just trust me."

Malia bowed her head. "Okay. I'll try."

The librarian returned with the treasure box. "You seem like you're on your way someplace important. Would you like to take it with you now, or just look inside for a moment?"

"Just for a moment, please." Suddenly, hope burned bright inside Malia. What if the CD had found its way back into the box? It wouldn't be the strangest thing that had happened so far.

But when she unlocked the box and lifted the cover,

all Malia found was another poem and a manila envelope. She was about to lock it all up and give it back when the librarian reached out to stop her.

"Anything inside is yours to keep." She smiled at Malia and her mom. "Who knows? Maybe it was meant for you."

Malia thought of her last two treasures—the painting that had shown her a new way to be happy, and the poem that had shown her how to be brave. Neither one of them had seemed like what she needed right away, but maybe these new treasures could help her not mess up her song in front of everybody at her brand-new school.

There was only one problem. "I don't have a treasure to leave. What will the next person get?"

"I'll take care of that, now that you showed me how to open it." The librarian gave Malia a wrinkly wink. "Don't worry, though. Your mother and I will keep the secret safe."

As they sped up the street, Malia saw her new school growing on the horizon. The construction mess was all cleaned up, and rows of chairs had been set up in front of a stage on the school's wide lawn.

Malia unpacked her harp beside the stage, then pulled out the new poem to settle her nerves. This time, she loved her treasure right away. It started out sad, but by the end, Malia knew the girl in the poem would be just fine. She almost felt like the girl in the poem could be *her*, and she wished she knew who had written it. She opened the big envelope, just to take a peek. But when she saw what was inside, she had to pull it all the way out.

There on the paper, delicately drawn, were the girl from the hospital and the girl from the restaurant—the other two who'd had the box. Malia was sure of it now. The picture seemed almost chalky, but not like the chalk she used so clumsily on the restaurant board. She slid it back into the envelope. *I can't keep this. It must have been left by mistake.* She'd take it to the lost and found drawer at the library tomorrow.

Or maybe not. When Malia looked up from the envelope, she stopped. There, setting up the very last long, straight row of chairs, was the girl from the restaurant—and the picture. Malia started down the aisle as her heart tugged her toward the girl.

"Hey. Does this belong to you?"

Her eyes lit up before she'd even opened the envelope. "Yes! Thanks! I can't believe you're here. I was going to draw you at the top." She looked up at Malia. "Wait, how did you know it wasn't treasure I left on purpose?"

Already, it felt like they were sharing a secret language. "I just knew, I guess."

"Did you get the other paintings?"

"I got one painting, a couple of weeks ago."

"Of the colorful neighborhood?"

"Yes! That's the one!" Malia's heart beat hard and fast. "Did you get my CD? Do you have it here? Maybe my performance won't be a disaster after all!"

The girl shook her head. "Sorry. I never got a CD, just a poem and a flyer with a song on the bottom." She really did look sorry, but Malia's heart sank all the same. She was glad the girl had gotten the song, but that wasn't the treasure she needed right now.

Miss Rousseau motioned for Malia to join her at the front, but she couldn't leave just yet. "Hey, do you think you could teach me to draw like that?"

The girl shrugged one shoulder. "Maybe. But Mel could for sure. She's the art teacher. Sign up for drawing and we'll be in the same class!"

Malia smiled. She'd always wished she were a better

artist. She already knew the first thing she'd draw: a butterfly for Hope's nursery. "I'll sign up for drawing if you'll sign up for choir. My mom wants me to learn other instruments, but we can't really afford any after buying my harp."

"Deal." The girl reached out and gave Malia's hand a firm shake. "I'm Jada, by the way. I'm glad you didn't vanish for good after that fire alarm."

Malia laughed. "I'm Malia. And I'm sorry about the fire alarm. Come back and we'll give you guys a free lunch to make up for it."

Jada bounced on her toes. "Yes! It's a deal. You guys have the best food in Utah." Jada tucked her painting back into the envelope. "Come find me after and I'll show you the school. But right now you'd better get onstage before that lady has a heart attack."

Malia agreed. She rushed toward the stage and the panicked Miss Rousseau, but still, she felt a connection to Jada. Like the string of a harp, pulled tight.

As Malia slid into her seat, Jada flashed her a thumbs-up from the back row, and Malia gave her a little wave. She closed her eyes and fingered the strings of an invisible harp as people settled in around her. Somehow she had to remember the notes.

A woman in a plain gray dress stepped to the microphone. "Welcome, students, parents, and community members, to our Back to School Night. Since tonight is all about getting to know each other, we've asked just a few students to perform for you, and then you're welcome to wander through the school and enjoy some refreshments."

The woman glanced back toward the few students onstage. "We'll begin the program with a recitation by Grace Andrews. Grace will be sharing an original poem tonight, and I think it speaks to this time in your lives when you'll all be seeking new friends. Grace?"

Once the girl stood, Malia had to blink twice to be sure of what she was seeing.

It's the girl from the hospital. The other girl from the picture.

Grace squared her shoulders and stepped to the microphone. "My poem is called 'Friendship Lost and Friendship Found.'"

As Malia glanced down at the paper in her own hand—the treasure she'd just found in the box—Grace spoke exactly the same lines Malia was reading. Her words were soft at first, and some in the audience leaned forward to hear, but by the end, Grace spoke strong and clear.

"I lost my voice and my best friend too
On swift, fierce winds and wings of blue,
The cold rain fell where beams had shone,
So I wrapped up tight and safe. Alone.

But I missed my friend, I missed my voice,
And my heart still whispered of another choice
To break out of my binding, dark, safe, and warm,
And see what the world looked like after the storm.

So I struggled free and was greeted by
Colorful brushstrokes across the sky,
The melody of the summer breeze
And blue wings like mine in hazel trees.

On the soft, sweet air of the mountain glade,
We gathered together in cool, green shade,
And told our stories, beginnings to ends,
And found our song in the hearts of new friends."

The crowd applauded and the girl beamed as she took her seat. She drew a deep breath and let it out slowly, the smile still full on her face. As two taller girls stepped to the front of the stage and tuned their violins, Malia leaned across their now-empty seats and showed Grace the copy of the poem she'd found in the box.

Grace smiled shyly. "I'm glad you found the box at the hospital. I left it there by mistake, except now it doesn't feel like one." She paused. "Did you like my poem?"

"It's really good. You were brave up there." Malia felt the hope grow inside her again. "Are you the one who found my CD?" she whispered.

Grace nodded.

"Did you listen to the song?"

"About a hundred times." Grace smiled again. "Mostly with my mom."

Malia had an idea. When the crowd clapped for the violinists, she leaned over and asked Grace for her help. Grace only hesitated a moment before she agreed.

The woman in gray stepped back to the microphone. "We'll conclude our program with Bach's Prelude in C Major, performed by a talented young harpist, Malia Wood."

Malia stepped to the side of the stage where her harp

had been set up, and Grace followed. She picked up an empty chair and placed it just behind Malia.

As Malia tipped her harp back, Grace reached up and touched the M-W butterfly engraved on the neck. "I thought that might be you," she whispered.

Malia nodded. "That's me. Are you ready?"

"I'm ready." Grace pressed her lips together as Malia lifted her hands.

There were at least a hundred people in the audience, and three whole rows of them were Malia's own family. But Malia only looked at her mom, proud that she could play this song perfectly for her. Even though Malia was the only one who could hear Grace's quiet humming as her own arpeggios rose and fell over the crowd, she knew her performance was truly a duet. Most things, it turned out, really were better with two.

Or sometimes, she thought as she saw Jada rushing through the applauding crowd with the choir signup sheet in her hand, *they're best with three*.

The girls passed the paper and pen around and signed their names right next to each other—Grace, Jada, Malia. She didn't have to wonder anymore who the other treasure box girls really were or whether she'd see them again.

They'd see each other every day. After Malia drew her heart-butterfly initials beside her name, she felt a gentle squeeze on her shoulder.

It was her mom. "Sweetheart, that was perfect. I am so, so proud of you." She blinked back her tears, then brightened. "I almost forgot! I promised I'd bring something for the refreshment table. Would you girls go get it from the car?"

Malia felt grown-up as she took the keys and led Jada and Grace to her car. When they opened the back, Malia's heart soared.

Symmetrical swirls of icing covered the most beautiful chocolate cake Malia had ever seen, resting in the center of the cut-glass cake stand.

Her mom had remembered.

Jada gave a long, low whistle. "Do we have to share?"

Malia laughed as she lifted the cake from the back of the car.

"I can carry it," said Grace. "If you want." She took a deep breath. "And then maybe we can go explore the school together?"

Malia and Jada happily agreed. Grace carried the cake to the refreshment table and cut three thick slices. Then the girls settled themselves under a tree and ate soft, sweet bites of Malia's mother's cake as they told their stories—of their art, their families, and most of all, *Amicitia*, the box that had brought them together.

Epilogue

IT WAS COOLER now, even in the library, and the coffee shop upstairs had begun to smell like pumpkin and cinnamon. The old librarian fastened the buttons of her sweater. She inched her cart from the storage room, ready to begin the daily task of returning lonely children's books to their proper places.

As she passed the row of soft reading sofas, Hazel paused. There, curled up on one of the sofas, was the Andrews girl with the long red hair. *Grace, I believe.*

The librarian watched as Grace's fingers made careful creases in a sheet of sky blue origami paper. After she pressed the final fold into place, Grace held her creation at arm's length to admire it. The librarian started forward, wondering whether Grace would like to help shelve the books.

Just then, Grace turned toward the entrance with a wave and a smile. Two more girls had arrived, and Hazel recognized them at once. First the artist with the colorful jewelry, who certainly didn't seem to be in a Picasso mood anymore. Just behind her, the sweet musician with the sad eyes. But they shone brightly as she pulled a baby picture from her pocket.

The three girls rushed together with happy whispers and flushed cheeks. Hazel was sure they would have greeted each other with even more noise and excitement if they hadn't been in the library. They were certainly no longer lost. Not now that they had found each other.

After a few more giggles and whispers, the other two took their backpacks and headed for the reading attic. But

Grace lingered for a moment. She smiled as she placed her origami carefully on the table, then rushed to catch up with her friends.

Hazel left her cart to pick up the tiny blue shape. *A butterfly,* she thought. *How lovely.* She breathed a peaceful sigh. It really was beautiful, and she knew just the place for it.

The old librarian made her way to the back room and tucked the butterfly in the lost and found drawer, safe inside the treasure box. The box and the butterfly would both be there, if they were needed.

One by one, Hazel returned the books from her cart. As she did, she listened to the girls' quiet, happy chatter, feeling that everything, *everything,* was just as it should be.

Acknowledgments

THERE ARE MANY people who have had a hand in making this book a reality, and I'm so grateful for the chance to sing their praises.

First and foremost, thanks to my family:

Robbie, you've been endlessly supportive and encouraging along every step of my journey, in every aspect of my life. You are simply the best, yet somehow you just keep getting better.

Jack and Halle and Lucy, you're the reason I write and the very most inspiring and amazing people I know.

It would be impossible to thank my parents sufficiently for reading every manuscript, for watching my kids for countless hours, for loving and supporting me unconditionally, and for being my first and best teachers. I love you both so much.

Thanks to my siblings, Ally, Nic, and Hope, for your support and encouragement, and for making my childhood an awesome, happy adventure that I want to revisit in my stories.

Thanks to my incredible agent, Ammi-Joan Paquette, for believing in me and my work, for finding this book its perfect home, and for being one of the smartest, kindest, most admirable people I know.

Thanks to Emilia Rhodes for falling in love with this book and shaping it so beautifully. I am grateful for your guidance every day. Thank you to Jen Klonsky, Alice Jerman, Maya Packard, Alison Klapthor, Jessica Berg, and the entire team at Harper.

Thanks to Sara Not for bringing my girls to life.

Thanks to my incomparably awesome writing group: Rosalyn Eves, Tasha Seegmiller, Erin Shakespear, and Helen Boswell. You make every page better, every time. And to my other amazing readers: Kate Birch, Emily

Shrope, Jennifer Bertman, Jennifer Stewart, Ann Bedichek, Jeannie Mobley, Kari Ann Holt, Jenilyn Collings, Hayley Farris, Brooke MacNaughtan, Jenny Call, Bridget Lee (plus Rachel and Ian!), the whole Vickers family, and especially Becky Shrope, Jory Wilson, and Ilima Todd, for making sure I got these girls just right. Thank you to Trent Reedy and Amber McConnell for coming up with the perfect poem and quote right when I needed them.

Thanks to all the amazing teachers who helped me learn to write about and observe and love the world around me: Alice Braithwaite, Kathryn Ipson, Sara Penny, LuAnn Keate, Vicki Challis, Linda Wilson, Carol Ann Nyman, Janet Weaver, Harold Shirley, Steve Steffensen, Joel Miller, Ty Redd. And so many others.

Thank you to my huge extended writing family, including the EMLA Gangos and the Rock Canyon Writers. I feel so fortunate to be part of the kidlit community and am constantly amazed at all the talented, kind, hardworking people who want nothing more than to bring great stories for young people into the world.

Finally, thank you to all the readers, who know that good books are like magic too.

HOOKSETT PUBLIC LIBRARY
HOOKSETT, NH 03106 —
603.485.6092
http://hooksettlibrary.org